THE SUMMER OF THE HAUNTING

THE SUMMER OF
THE HAUNTING

William Corlett (signature)

William Corlett

For Colin,

a little night reading
for Christmas, '93!

With our love always

Bill + Bryan + Charlie
x

THE BODLEY HEAD
LONDON

First published in 1993

1 3 5 7 9 10 8 6 4 2

Copyright © William Corlett 1993

William Corlett has asserted his right under the Copyright,
Designs and Patents Act, 1988 to be identified as the author of
this work

First published in the United Kingdom in 1994
by The Bodley Head Children's Books
Random House, 20 Vauxhall Bridge Road, London SW1V 2SA

Random House Australia (Pty) Limited
20 Alfred Street, Milsons Point, Sydney,
New South Wales 2061, Australia

Random House New Zealand Limited
18 Poland Road, Glenfield,
Auckland 10, New Zealand

Random House South Africa (Pty) Limited
PO Box 337, Bergvlei 2012, South Africa

Random House UK Limited Reg. No. 954009

A CIP catalogue record for this book is available from the
British Library

ISBN 0 370 31819 6

Phototypeset by Intype, London

Printed in Great Britain by Mackays of Chatham PLC, Chatham, Kent

THE SUMMER OF THE HAUNTING

PART ONE

LONDON
(Talliser Road)

On the night before the haunting began Emma gave herself a tattoo. She had wanted one for almost a year, but it wasn't until she had broached the subject with her mother, Harriet, that what had at first seemed no more than a casual whim grew into an obsession. Harriet, of course, was absolutely opposed to the idea and they'd ended up having a particularly noisy row. Not that there was anything unusual about this. Recently they'd spent a lot of time rowing. Harriet said it was to do with Emma's age – she was approaching fifteen – but probably the fact that theirs was a single parent/only child relationship and that they spent so much time alone in each others company was the real reason. However, the tattoo issue brought them closer to a serious parting of the ways than anything that had come before. Emma had gone so far as to threaten to camp out on her father's doorstep and force him and wife-number-three to take her in and Harriet had yelled at her with a terrible bitterness that that was precisely the fate she deserved.

The following evening, spurred on by this continued animosity, Emma finally summoned up the courage to do the tattoo. She knew it was possible to give oneself some sort of 'personal mark' (as she preferred to think of it) with a needle and Indian ink. The brother of a school friend had once printed the letters H A T and E on the knuckles of his right hand and he had described the technique with boastful clarity to a circle of admirers, hoping to impress. At the time Emma had decided that if she gave herself a mark she would choose something more aesthetic than his crude message of violence – a bluebird appealed to her, perhaps, or a fully blown rose. But that evening, as she sat on the side of the bath, expediency and nervousness persuaded her to a more simple five pointed star. It would be located on her left shoulder, at the front, in the fleshy hollow between the shoulder blade and the collar bone. She chose this site partly because there she would be able to see it but also because doing the job herself limited the number of places that she was able to use.

Emma had the house to herself, Harriet having gone to visit her mother at Strand-on-the-Green. Once in the bathroom and with the door locked, she set out her tools for the job beside the basin. Then she removed her T-shirt and stared thoughtfully at her reflection in the mirror. The light in the bathroom was harsh and unkind. (Harriet refused to use the mirror there, preferring the softer reflection in her bedroom. 'The bathroom mirror may tell the truth,' she said, 'but who wants to know it?') Emma saw her lank, dark hair caught back with an elastic band. Her excuse for staying in had been to wash her hair and it certainly needed it. It was greasy and, because she was growing it having had a period when she'd kept it very short, it looked unkempt. Beneath it her face was too white in the harsh glare of the light. She looked pasty and plain.

4

She wrinkled her nose in disgust and stuck out her tongue at the stranger who stared back at her. Then, putting her hand on her bare shoulder, she felt the hollow where the tattoo would be. She shivered with anticipation and slid her hand down, covering her small round breast. Then, taking a deep breath, she turned on the taps and ran some water into the basin. Next she washed her hands. She felt like a surgeon or a priest at some strange pagan ceremony. She dried them on a towel and picking up the needle and thread she dipped it in the ink. Finally, with another deep inhalation of breath, she made the first mark.

As the needle pierced the skin a pain stabbed through her body, making her wince. Withdrawing the needle, she squinted down at her shoulder and then looked at her reflection in the mirror. There was an angry little red blotch, but the ink had failed to go in. Gritting her teeth, she immersed the needle in the ink once more and jabbed again at her flesh. This time she squeezed her thumb and forefinger against the cotton pushing it towards the end of the needle. Again she removed the needle. Her finger and thumb were stained with ink. She ran more hot water into the basin and rubbed at the marks with a pumice stone. Then she looked at her shoulder again. The angry inflamed spot – like a midge bite – now had a black centre. As she saw this first vestige of her tattoo, a shiver ran down her back making her straighten up and shake her head. She looked at her reflection again. Her eyes met the eyes in front of her, holding the look. Well, she thought, I'm doing it at last. And in her head she heard the mocking voice that she dreaded so much whisper back: 'Who's a clever girl then? Who's a clever girl?'

Emma shook her head, banishing the voice. She knew it of old. It mimicked her and mocked her and usually occurred when she was alone and low.

'Get lost!' she said, defiantly. Then, picking up the needle and thread once more, she continued to introduce the five points of the star onto her previously unblemished shoulder.

When Harriet returned she found Emma sitting in a dressing gown with a towel over her head watching television and eating a bowl of cereal.

'You all packed?' she asked, pouring herself a drink.

'Yep!' Emma replied, lifting the spoon to her mouth and not taking her eyes off the screen.

'What's that on your hand?'

Emma glanced down at her stained fingers.

'Ink,' she replied in a bored, casual tone. 'I was doing a drawing.'

'Any good?' Harriet asked, sitting in one of the armchairs and taking a gulp of whisky.

'Not bad,' Emma replied.

'Can I see it?'

'I threw it away.' Emma replied and, as she lied, she looked at her mother and smiled.

Then she turned away again. Her shoulder was throbbing and sore. She had an overwhelming desire to cry and she didn't really know why.

'You all right?' her mother asked her, kindly.

'Yeah!' Emma replied. But in fact she felt sad and lonely. The pain in her shoulder was stinging and hot. It seemed to emphasize a gulf that separated her not only from her mother but also from herself – the self that she had been before the tattoo.

'I'm going to bed,' she said and, getting up, she hurried out of the room.

DIARY

I've done it. Shoulder very sore. Hope I haven't poisoned it or given myself gangrene or something. But I'm glad it's done. It makes me feel different already. Mother returned looking flushed again. I'm sure she's up to something that she's not telling me about. It's so pathetic that she thinks I care what she does when I don't really care about anything. We leave for Yorkshire first thing in the morning. If life continues to be this uneventful I shall stop keeping a diary. This one certainly would NOT provide 'something sensational to read on a train journey'.

PART TWO

YORKSHIRE
(Borthwick Hall)

One

1

The first view of the house was from high up. The road swung round a corner and, dropping slightly, entered a thick wood of stunted oaks, their tops singed by the sharp wind that blew in from the coast on even the hottest of summer days. All the way across the moor the sea was visible as a thin band of dark on the horizon. The breeze had been brisk and chill, the sun dazzling. But now, as the road started its descent into the dale, the temperature became warmer and the light was filtered through a screen of branches and leaves, infusing everything with a soft green haze.

'Nearly there!' Harriet said, changing gear as the road turned and dipped more steeply. Then, rounding a corner, the valley bottom and the house came into view.

'That's it!' Harriet exclaimed and she braked, stopping at the side of the lane, so that Emma could get a proper look.

The house was large, but not excessively so. It was built of red brick that had mellowed over the years to the colour of burnt sand. It had a tiled roof above a stone pediment and tall chimneys surmounted by elongated pots. There were a number of dormer windows set high into the roof with below them two rows of well proportioned sash windows, painted a gleaming white and with stonework surrounds. At the centre of the ground floor, glass double doors opened onto a broad terrace that descended by steps to well-kept lawns and flower beds. The grounds of the house, which looked extensive, were separated from the neighbouring pasture land by brick walls on either side and by an elaborate wrought iron fence and gateway along the front. Beyond, out in the meadow, the waters of a pool surrounded by trees glinted in the sunlight. A few cows munched in their shade or lay in languid heaps, tails flicking at flies.

'That's actually the back of the house. The front drive and main entrance faces the other direction – up the valley,' Harriet explained.

'Isn't there any village?' Emma asked.

'Further down, towards the bottom end of the dale. About a couple of miles away. Not that it's much of a village. A shop, a church, a pub and a few houses. That's about all.'

'What do people do?'

'Mainly farming, I suppose.'

'No. I meant for entertainment.'

'I've no idea.' Harriet's tone made it clear she thought Emma was being tiresome. 'What do people do in the country? I expect they hunt and shoot and fish. Please don't begin complaining already.' She started the engine up again and the car continued the descent into the valley.

'I shan't say another word,' Emma muttered morosely.

The view of the house came and went as they

twisted and turned along the wooded hillside. Each time it reappeared it was appreciably closer; each time more details were evident.

'It's certainly a beautiful place,' Harriet murmured, more to herself than to her daughter. 'A very beautiful place.'

Emma stared at the building sourly.

'What's so special about it?' she asked in a bored voice.

'It's a Queen Anne gem!' Harriet replied.

'Oh, mother!'

'What?' the note of irritation creeping back into her voice.

Emma pursed her lips and bit back a bad-tempered reply. If they were to survive the next two weeks together without murder being committed she decided it would be wisest not to start rowing before they'd even arrived.

'What's wrong with the place anyway?' she asked instead.

'Wrong? Nothing's wrong with it,' Harriet replied, still tetchy.

'There must be something that needs doing for Lady Thing to get you in.'

'Oh, I see,' Harriet said, with a degree of apology in her voice for her earlier misplaced irritability. 'There's nothing actually wrong with it. Just some rooms that need attention. Messed about by the Victorians – all heavy red wood panelling and over-elaborate cornices. The Shawcrosses quite rightly want them restored.'

'You mean rag rolling and Roman blinds?'

'Cheeky!' Harriet exclaimed, but she did at least smile as she said it. 'Actually it's more a case of stripping away what's there. . . . But I dare say there'll be the odd tasteful paint job as well. I've already fixed up with two local chaps to do the building and carpentry.'

'So what is "Harriet Charrington, Designer To The Stars" going to be doing all day?'

'Everything else!' Harriet replied firmly.

'Well – I hope Lord Thing is seriously rich – because you don't come cheap, do you?'

'Certainly not! I should hate to be thought of as cheap. And he isn't a lord, Em. I've told you. He's Sir Michael Shawcross. The chairman of Shawcross International.'

'I don't know what that is, do I?'

'Yes, you do. They make computers and run hotels and airlines. . . . They have that commercial on TV at the moment. The one with the guy swimming down Fifth Avenue. . . .'

'So Lord Thing is rich?'

'SIR Michael? Yes. Very. This is only one of his several houses.'

'How disgusting. There are people sleeping in boxes on the streets of our cities, you know.'

'So? What's Michael Shawcross supposed to do about it?'

'The rich should be taxed – to pay for the poor.'

'They are. Even I am. If you're going to wear your bourgeois little socialist heart on your sleeve, I'll wish I'd left you at home with your grandmother. . . .'

They had reached the valley bottom and come, by way of a narrow leafy lane, to a place where wrought iron gates were set back from the road. Here a long straight gravel drive passed between two rows of chestnut trees with black metal fences separating them from the pastures beyond. At the

14

end of this avenue, the drive went over a cattle grid and through more wrought iron gates before arriving at a flagged forecourt and the front of Borthwick Hall. This side of the house was shaped like a flattened 'E' – with two wings and, at the centre, a protruding porch with a large window above it.

The second set of gates was closed and Harriet had to stop the car in front of them. For a moment neither she nor Emma spoke. They stared at the house expectantly, hoping for someone to appear.

'Shouldn't a serf rush out to greet us?' Emma asked.

'Some sign of life would be reassuring,' Harriet agreed. 'Would it be rude to honk the horn?'

'You're a terrible snob, mother. You really care what Lord and Lady Thing think about you.'

'Of course I don't,' Harriet snapped – but she grabbed at Emma's hand as she leaned across and planted it firmly on the horn. 'Stop it! Em! It's a horrible noise.'

The horrible noise, however, had little effect. Still no one came to open the gates.

'It does look ominously vacant,' Harriet said, peering at the distant heavily curtained windows, each one of them shut in spite of the warm weather.

'You are sure we're expected?' Emma asked, brightly.

'Of course we are. You've seen the letter yourself. Everything was fixed when I came to show them the designs. Try the gates, darling.'

Emma got out of the car and walked over to the wrought iron gates. They wouldn't budge. She held the heavy handle with both hands and tried to turn it.

'It's no use,' she called. 'They're locked.' Then

leaning against the ornate metal she stared at the house. It seemed so particularly still and silent, almost as if it were waiting or as if, behind the curtains, hidden eyes were looking out and watching her. Emma shivered, feeling suddenly cold although the sun was still shining and the evening air held in the shelter of the valley was warm and breathless.

'What shall we do?' her mother asked as she got out of the car and crossed to join her.

'Find somewhere to have supper,' Emma replied. 'I'm starving.' Then, as she was turning back towards the car, a sudden flash of light caught her attention from a first floor window on the corner of the left-hand wing.

'What was that?' she exclaimed.

'What?' Harriet asked.

'Don't know.' Emma shook her head and frowned, searching the window. 'I thought I saw something move . . . in that window on the corner.' She pointed, as she spoke, indicating the window to her mother. They both stared eagerly, hoping for a welcoming wave or at least an enquiring face to look out.

'Can't see anything now,' Emma said, disappointment making her sound sulky. Her shoulder had started throbbing again. She wondered if she had poisoned herself.

'Where?' Harriet insisted, still searching the house for signs of life.

'I was mistaken, Mother. Whatever it was, it's gone now,' Emma snapped, irritably.

'A ghost!' Harriet joked. Then, rattling the gates, she called out: 'Hello! Anyone at home? Hello!'

Rooks cawed in distant trees and a few birds sang.

'Nothing!' Harriet said with disgust. 'No one. The place is empty!' Then, as she turned towards the car, a sudden thought made her look back again. 'That's one of the rooms I'm supposed to be working on.'

'Which is?' Emma asked.

'The window where you thought you saw something.' Harriet leaned against the car and looked at her watch. 'This is ridiculous and bloody annoying.'

'Language, mother dear!'

'Well – we've just had a very long drive. . . .'

'Here's someone now,' Emma called, stopping Harriet in mid-sentence. A woman had appeared from round the side of the house and was walking across the paved forecourt towards them.

Harriet hurried back and stood beside Emma. They both stared at the woman, feeling slightly foolish with the locked gates barring their entrance.

'It's Mrs Charrington, is it?' the woman called as she got closer.

'Ms,' Harriet said, crisply. 'Ms Charrington. It isn't my married name.'

The woman looked perplexed for a moment then shrugged.

'But you are the Harriet Charrington who's expected? The decorator woman?'

Harriet nodded. 'Can you let us in, please?' she asked, irritation growing in her voice.

'I was beginning to worry,' the other woman said, ignoring this request. 'Thought you might be lost.'

'We weren't due 'til five,' Harriet said, checking her watch again, 'it's only half past.'

'Not to worry,' the woman said with a smile.

17

'Is Lady Shawcross here?' Harriet asked, her voice stiff and formal.

'No – they went yesterday. She's always changing her plans. She's left all your instructions with me.'

'And you are . . . ?'

'Lynda Carver. I'm the housekeeper.'

The two women stared at each other through the bars of the gate, sizing each other up. Then Harriet smiled, a brief, cold smile.

'The main drive is only in use when the family are at home,' the woman continued. 'You were meant to come to the side gate. Down to the lane and along to the left. You can't miss it.'

'Can't we come in this way now we're here?' Emma asked.

'As you can see, everything's locked up, love,' Mrs Carver said and although she smiled she didn't seem very friendly.

'We'll come round then,' Harriet said getting back into the car and, as Emma climbed in beside her, she added in a low voice; 'This is not a good beginning.'

2

Lynda Carver had at least prepared food for them – or so she said when she admitted them into the house through the side door.

'I've left a casserole for your supper this evening,' she told them as she lead them along a hallway towards a dark, narrow staircase. 'But I won't be doing the cooking from now on. Not once you're settled in. I don't do cooking. Not even for the family. Right, I'll take you up to your rooms first

18

then, when you come down, I'll show you where everything else is.'

The staircase led to a short landing at the end of which closed double doors blocked the way.

'That's the way into the main part of the house. Where you'll be working. You've been given beds in what used to be the servants' quarters – next flight up.'

'Do you live in, Mrs Carver?' Harriet asked, her voice sounding pinched and truculent, peeved at the reference to servants' quarters.

'Good God, no! You wouldn't catch me living in. Too big! Any road, I've got a family of my own to look after – my husband's away, working on the rigs, but there are the kids and the old man. Besides, I like my freedom too much. If I lived in Lady Shawcross would have me working all hours. She has a nanny and an old couple who do the cooking and odd jobs – they go everywhere with them. Can't call their lives their own. No thank you! Not me! I live down in the village – out of harm's way – and I come in each day, Monday to Friday, nine-thirty till four-thirty. So you can see, I'm well past my usual time now.' They reached the next landing. Here, another door separated the stairs from a passage which ran the length of the house with a number of rooms opening off both sides of it. It was a dark, gloomy corridor, lit only by one small window at the far end. Lynda Carver walked ahead of them.

'These rooms are mostly for the staff,' she said, 'and extra guests, of course. The amount of entertaining they do, you would not believe. They spend more in one weekend than I earn in a year. . . .' Then, as she neared the end of the corridor, she opened a door as she passed it, and called over her shoulder. 'This is your lavatory and your bathroom's just next to it, here.' She threw open another door, revealing a narrow, white-painted room, with a bath along one wall and a basin beneath a dormer window. 'The water's heated by an immersion – on a thermostat – so you don't need to worry about it. This is one of the bedrooms,' she continued, opening the door next to the bathroom, 'and the other is just opposite.'

The first bedroom was a good-sized, square room, with a low ceiling and rough plaster walls, painted white. Pale, floral curtains were looped back in folds from the dormer window and the material matched the spreads on the twin beds that took up most of the space along one of the side walls. Opposite was a dressing table, with a mirror and a lamp on either side of it. A chest of drawers was canted across one corner by the window and a wardrobe stood beside the door. A comfortable padded armchair was positioned near the window so as to maximize the light with a small table beside it.

'This will do fine,' Harriet said, putting her case down and walking over to look out of the window. The view was to the front of the house, with the paved courtyard and the closed and locked iron gates behind which they had waited on first arrival. Beyond them she could see the avenue of chestnuts stretching to the road.

'I'm glad you like it,' Lynda Carver said with a thin smile. Then turning to Emma she continued. 'You'll have the other room, then,' and led her across the corridor. The room they now entered was similar in size and in layout to the one Harriet had chosen. But here there was a second door on the side wall.

'This used always to be the governess' room in the olden days. There's a flight of steps behind that door that leads down to the nursery on the floor below. That's one of the rooms your mother will be working on. Though I can't think why they want to mess about with it. I like the wood panelling – it saves you having to keep redecorating.'

As she was speaking, Emma crossed over to this second door and turned the handle.

'It's locked, love. Keys in the door – but there's no need for you to use it. They're very steep steps. The family always keeps this door and the one at the bottom locked. Don't want a nasty accident, do we? Unless they have extra guests staying, of course. Then they sometimes use that staircase to get up here. Well, they wouldn't want to use the servant's stairs, would they? Right then, I hope you'll be very comfortable,' Lynda Carver added, changing the subject abruptly.

Emma turned and looked around her. This room contained a double bed in place of the two single ones across the corridor. The curtains here were of a different material and the view, when she went to the window, was over the gardens to the distant pond in the meadow with the valley dropping and disappearing into a haze of evening light beyond. But apart from that there was no difference between the two rooms – they were both identically feature-less and bland.

'Yes, it'll be fine,' Emma said in a bored voice.

'Good. That's settled then. Unless, of course, your mother would prefer the double bed?' Lynda Carver observed, eyeing Emma inquisitively.

21

'I don't suppose she'll be sleeping with anyone while she's here,' Emma said, still looking out of the window and with her back to the woman.

'I thought perhaps your dad might be coming up.'

'God! I should run for cover if he does!' Emma replied, a malicious gleam in her eye. 'They've been divorced since I was born.'

'Oh dear!' Lynda Carver said, obviously embarrassed by this unexpected confidence.

'Yes!' Emma exclaimed, turning to look at her with a bright smile. 'I think the shock of my arrival was more than he could bear! Still, he hasn't done badly since. He got two sons from his second marriage and now there's a baby girl from number three. And they're only the kids we all know about. There are probably others dotted about the place. He's very potent, my father. Very fecund! And, of course, ecologically hopeless. I don't think he's ever even heard of the condom, let alone used one.'

'Well, I'll just . . .' Lynda Carver murmured, backing out into the corridor, a pale pink blush suffusing her cheeks. 'I'll be down in the kitchen,' she called to Harriet as she hurried away. 'I'll make you a pot of tea. . . .'

As soon as she was alone Emma smiled and sat down on the side of the bed, hugging herself with pleasure. Lovely how speaking the truth could be so embarrassing for people, she thought. It shocked them. Shocking people like Lynda Carver, tight, buttoned-up people with thin lips that matched their narrow lives, gave Emma the greatest pleasure. Not that she knew anything about the woman, really. But there was something about the way she had pried into Harriet's and Emma's pri-

22

vate lives that made Emma instantly dislike her. She shrugged. Why should I let her get to me? she thought. She doesn't feature in my life. In a couple of weeks we'll be out of here and I won't even remember her name. Getting up she crossed to the dressing table and, unbuttoning her shirt, she inspected her shoulder where the little black star was surrounded by an area of puffy red skin.

'Is your room all right?' Harriet asked, coming in without warning.

Emma quickly closed her shirt and crossed to the window.

'I've got the double bed,' she said. 'D'you want it?'

'I don't suppose I'll be sleeping with anyone while I'm here, darling!' Harriet replied, making her voice light.

'That's what I just said to that ghastly woman,' Emma said, her back to her mother as she leaned out of the small window.

'Emma! You're not to upset the natives. Is she ghastly?'

'Nosy,' Emma replied. 'She wanted to know if my "dad" would be joining us.'

'You didn't say who he was, did you?' Harriet's voice sounded anxious.

'Why are you so ashamed of him?' Emma asked, knowing the answer.

'I'm not,' Harriet replied. 'It's just so boring. People think that because he's a "film star",' she said the words with a mocking tone as though they were in inverted commas, 'he must be some kind of god!'

'If God is anything like my father,' Emma

observed, 'I suddenly understand why the world's in such trouble!'

'Quite!' Harriet agreed, a touch too enthusiastically. Then, after a pause, she added, 'I'm going down. I want to check that all the materials and paints have been delivered. Everything was supposed to arrive this morning. There's a cup of tea being made,' and Emma heard her footsteps dissolving into the distance.

Alone once more, she turned and surveyed the room. It was excessively bright and cheerful; white walls and crisp white woodwork, matching lamp shades in that colour ubiquitously named 'old rose', with a darker carpet and a paler bedspread. A pink and white room; the sort of room that appears in those style magazines that Emma's mother subscribed to and which often contained examples of her own work. A room that would not merit a full page spread but would be one of a series of smaller photographs with some brief caption – 'a guest room at the top of the house'. An empty, sterile room, neat and clean, unlived in, unloved. A place rarely if ever visited by the owners of the house but kept aired and waiting in case of extra, unexpected guests.

That's what we are, Emma thought, visitors. People who don't belong here. Intruders.

The thought made her shiver, although the room was warm. She turned and looked again out of the window. The sun was flooding the valley with its late, golden lights. Rooks were massing in the trees by the distant pond. It was a tranquil, gentle scene.

Her hand involuntarily reached up and massaged the wound on her shoulder. She wondered if the village shop would sell TCP ointment. Then, crossing to the door she went out into the corridor.

As Emma started down the stairs a sudden noise made her swing round. It was her bedroom door slamming shut behind her.

She did for a moment think it strange that it should have happened, because there was not a breath of air stirring along the corridor, but then her attention was caught up again by her new surroundings and any vague suspicion about the strangeness of the event went out of her head.

3

Lynda Carver was obviously in a hurry to get home.

'My old dad lives with us and he gets in a right state if he doesn't have his tea on time.'

She showed them where everything was that they might need in the kitchen and then took them through to a sitting room at the front of the house.

'Lady Shawcross says you can use it,' she explained, almost grudgingly. 'It's the family's TV room. You can't get through the evenings without a bit of telly, can you? Mind, all the other rooms on this floor are locked up – and so are the principal bedrooms. You can't be too careful – not with workmen in the house. I've just left the rooms you'll be working on open. All the furniture has been moved out. I had to get that done this week . . .'

'I'll need to know where it is,' Harriet cut in.

'Of course,' Lynda Carver replied evenly. 'You just say when you want it. It's all in one of the outhouses. I must get off. I'll be back in the morning. I do more work when they're away on holiday than when they're here. She wants all the curtains taken down and sent to the cleaners. Covers off the sofas and chairs. The lot. They have it done every year. That's money for you! She says it makes things last longer. I've got a sofa that was covered for our wedding and it's still going strong. Any little mark – I just dab at it with a sponge and some washing-up liquid. Still, that's what it's like in this country. . . . The rich man in his castle, the poor man at his gate . . . You'll know how to use that telly? It's not very good reception on account of the house being so deep in the valley. I told them to get one of those discs – they could afford it. But apparently it wouldn't go with the architecture of the house, or so Madam says . . .' and still talking she hurried back to the kitchen and when Harriet and Emma caught up with her she was already getting her car keys out of her bag. 'I hope you'll be very comfortable.' she said, continuing towards the open back door. 'See you in the morning.' Then she was gone and a moment later they heard a car starting up.

'She doesn't exactly make you feel welcome, does she?' Emma said wandering back into the kitchen.

'Country folk,' Harriet said, in an exaggerated North Country voice. 'We don't trust strangers up here!' Then in her own voice she added. 'Let's eat. You were right. I'm starving.'

The casserole was basic but quite tasty. They had it sitting opposite each other at the kitchen table and afterwards washed up at the shallow stone sink beneath a window looking out onto the big, square yard surrounded by outhouses and stables, through which an arch gave access to the side drive up which they had been forced to arrive.

26

While Emma was finishing the drying-up Harriet went on what she called 'a booze hunt'.

'They must have a left a bottle of gin tucked away somewhere!' she remarked, going out of the room. 'After all, we were told to use the house as our own.'

Later Emma heard her cry out triumphantly 'Eureka!' and she returned with gin, tonic and a large bottle of diet coke.

'They have an entire room full of bottles!' she said with a grin. 'I'd better put it on a time lock or I'll spend the days pissed!'

They watched television until after The Nine O'Clock News and then Harriet said she was shattered by the drive and was going to bed.

'I'll have an early start in the morning. The builders are arriving at eight . . .'

The sound of a telephone ringing stopped her in mid-sentence. There was a receiver in the room on a table near to where Emma was curled up on the sofa. For a moment they looked at each other, surprised by this familiar sound in such unfamiliar surroundings, then Emma reached out and answered it.

'The Shawcross establishment,' she said, in a mock posh voice then she pulled a face. 'Just a minute, I'll get her. It's for you. Mother dear,' she said sweetly for the benefit of whoever was at the other end of the line and held out the receiver.

'Who is it?' Harriet whispered.

'Lady Shawcross!' Emma mouthed and started to giggle.

'Hello,' Harriet said into the telephone. Then added, 'Yes!', after listening for several moments to the animated voice, 'she'll make a very good social secretary!' and she pulled a face at Emma. 'We're fine. Oh, please don't worry! We'll get our own drink in. . . . Well – the odd gin and tonic might cheer the end of the day. . . . Oh, how kind!. . . . I'm sure I'll find it. . . . Yes, she was here to greet us. . . . No. She made us a casserole . . . To tell you the truth we were just on our way to bed. It's been a long day. . . . Have a good holiday. . . . When you return it'll all be finished. . . . Goodbye, Lady Shawcross. . . . Oh, thank you. Well then – good-bye, Lavinia.'

After the call Harriet went up to bed, leaving Emma watching a film which they had both already seen.

'It's the one with that horrible scene where she breaks both his ankles with a sledge hammer,' Harriet said through a yawn as she crossed to the door.

'Thanks, Mother! If I hadn't already seen it, that would really have ruined it for me.'

'But you have, so why not come to bed?'

'I'm not tired yet,' Emma complained.

'Well, don't stay up all night, darling . . .' Harriet said, going out.

Emma sat staring moodily at the set while around her the dusk gathered until the only light left in the room came from the flickering images on the screen. The fact that she had seen the film before and that therefore the shocks were not as powerful, had a deadening effect. That and the long drive from London made her drowsy and soon she was finding it difficult to keep awake. The picture on the television finally blurred over and when next she opened her eyes the film was almost at an end.

For a moment Emma couldn't remember where

28

she was. The unfamiliar room flickered and strobed in the light from the television set. Dark corners hid strange secrets, so foreign and unrecognizable were her surroundings to her. Outside the window the pitch night flattened itself against the glass. The country silence was thick as a blanket round her, punctuated only by the soundtrack of the film with its incongruous, brash stridence. Emma felt hemmed in by the unfamiliar blankness of the place. An oppressive claustrophobia made her gasp for breath as though the darkness and silence were a physical wall closing about her, squeezing her tight, pressing in on every side.

Rising quickly, she crossed to a standard lamp and, fumbling under the shade, found the switch. A pale, golden glow spilled out into the room restoring some order to her mind as the light cast explanations into the darkness, revealing armchairs and tables where moments before there had been unnamed shadows and unreal substance.

Emma shivered. She felt cold and clammy at the same time. Crossing, she switched off the television. The silence was absolute. It seemed to reverberate around her, throbbing in rhythm to her pulse beat. She hurried to the door and went out, leaving the standard lamp on. It wasn't that she had forgotten to switch it off but to have done so would have been to plunge the room back into darkness and that, at that moment, she was not prepared to do.

The stairwell was lit by weak electric bulbs with opaque glass shades. Emma hurried up the steps, three at a time, and arrived, breathless and with her heart pounding, at the top landing. Here there were two switches. One doused the bulbs on the stairs, the other illuminated three hanging lights along the length of the corridor. By their fitful glimmer Emma hurried to her room at the far end of the house. Once inside and with her own overhead light switched on she leaned against the door and gasped for breath. She was surprised to find that she was trembling and that her heart was beating too fast.

Stupid! she thought and crossed to turn on a bedside lamp. Then, after switching off the overhead light, she pulled off her clothes and folded them in a pile on the armchair. The room, in the meagre light from the lamp, looked cosy and calm. But Emma was still breathless and shaking.

'What is the matter with you?' the voice whispered in her head. 'Scared of the dark, Em?'

This head voice had plagued Emma for as long as she could remember. It whispered and mocked and gleefully undermined her, sometimes commenting on what she was doing, or repeating her words after her in a singsong, whining tone. It wasn't always there, of course, just on occasions – usually when she was depressed or lonely or when the world seemed against her. Then she would hear it murmuring in her head, copying and ridiculing her, enjoying the discomfort it caused. As though another Emma was there, an unfriendly, spiteful, alter ego.

Now, shaking her head to silence it, she went to the window. Bats were swooping below the roof line and thin clouds surrounded a half moon. Somewhere an owl hooted. Then the silence closed in again. As she leaned on the sill of the open window the night air felt cold on her naked body. Only her shoulder was hot and throbbing.

Crossing to the dressing table and switching on

a lamp beside the mirror she stared at her reflection. The skin round the little black star was red and angry. With a finger she massaged the area gently. Then, looking up, she stared deep into her own eyes.

'This is me,' she said out loud to her reflection and, as she spoke, she pointed at the tattoo. 'My distinguishing mark. This is me!' She felt a sudden fierce anger. This happened sometimes. For no apparent reason an overwhelming rage against the world would consume her. It made her mean and violent. On such occasions she wanted to smash things, to behave unkindly. She had once, in one of these moods, broken one of her grandmother's best teacups. She had actually snapped off the handle as she held the delicate china cup in her hands. No sooner had she done it than she was sorry but at the time, as her finger and thumb tightened on the thin handle, she had sensed an exhilarating surge of fury and glee and power. The power was almost frightening. When in its grip she felt she could do . . . anything. Now, as this familiar anger broke over her, she rose quickly, switched off the dressing table lamp and running across the room she climbed into bed.

As she switched off the bedside lamp she heard somebody laughing – a light, mocking sound, high and echoing. But of course at that time Emma still thought it was the voice in her head. It wasn't until later that she knew she was being haunted.

DIARY

Should have filled this in last night – but I fell asleep. Dreary evening watching television – nothing but repeats – after a long drive up here.

31

The house is large and rich and has a funny feeling about it – like a hotel without any guests. It is also a bit creepy. I wouldn't like to be here on my own. There's a housekeeper called Lynda, but she doesn't live in. So I'm quite glad Mother's here. Lynda has taken an instant dislike to me – which is reciprocated. She obviously disapproves of us. I must give her something really scandalous to work on. Anyway now it's morning and I'm going down to breakfast. Isn't this a riveting read?

Two

1

The builders had arrived by the time Emma went downstairs. Their names were Tom and Bill and they'd brought two other men with them to help with the heavy work – or so Tom told her. He was slight and fair, with his hair in a pony tail. Bill was taller and his hair was short and black and continued down his face into a trendy, stubbly beard and moustache.

They were all in the kitchen drinking mugs of tea when Emma appeared from the back stairs.

'Oh yes! It's all right for some!' a big, strapping lad with a beer gut announced as she walked into the room.

Her mother was nowhere to be seen.

'She's gone into Helmsley to see the woman who's making the curtains. She said she'll be back later,' Tom told her. Then he did the introductions. The lad with the beer gut was called Gary and the fourth man, who was older than the other three and had a finger missing on his right hand, was called Hank. He looked as if he'd just got back from a heavy drinking session. He nodded at Emma morosely and swilled his tea round in his mug, stirring in the sugar. As he did so Emma noticed a fading tattoo on his forearm. At once her shoulder started to throb as though in recognition of a kindred spirit. Startled and repulsed by this connection, Emma moved away, turning her back on him.

'Oh dear!' Hank said, in a mocking voice. 'She's shy!'

'Shut up, Hank!' Bill said. Then, turning, he smiled at Emma. 'D'you want some tea? It's just freshly made.'

'Don't mind,' Emma replied, feeling herself blushing.

'So what are you going to be doing all day?' Tom asked her, pouring tea into a mug.

Emma shrugged. She was conscious that they were all staring at her, full of open curiosity. The blood burnt her cheeks and her neck felt hot. 'I expect I'll go out and play!' she said, in a pretend, little girl voice, trying to sound jokey. Then, turning her back again to hide her blushing, she cut herself a slice of bread to toast.

'Come on, we'd best get back,' Tom said, crossing to the door. 'Let Emma have her breakfast in peace.'

'I haven't finished,' Hank complained.

'Well, bring it with you,' Tom called from the back hall.

Gary, who had been sitting on the kitchen table reading the sports page of his newspaper, was the last to leave.

'If you get bored,' he told her, with a broad wink, 'you can always turn to me for comfort!'

Emma ignored him, busying herself watching her toast under the grill. But as soon as they'd gone, she straightened up, her face hot with blushing and her heart racing. She walked over to the sink and, running the cold tap, she splashed water on her cheeks and ran her wet hands through her hair. Then she looked out of the window at the sun-baked yard.

A terrible sense of loneliness engulfed her. The day stretched ahead with nothing to do and nowhere to go. She sensed all the other days, an endless procession of boredom that lay ahead of her. She'd told her mother she didn't want to come for just this reason – but as usual Harriet hadn't bothered to listen. 'Mother never listens. She's so obsessed with being upwardly mobile that she doesn't give a toss about me,' Emma grumbled to herself. 'I mean what does she expect me to do while she's swanning about being Designer of the Year?'

'Selfish cow,' the voice in her head whispered, winding her up gleefully.

The smell of burning reminded her she was making toast and she hurried back to the stove. Smoke was issuing from the grill. She switched it off and pulled out the pan. The bread was black and one corner was on fire. Blowing on the flames, she picked up the charred remains and dropped them into the waste bin by the sink. Wetting a cloth, she returned to the stove and wiped the grill pan. She cut herself another slice of bread and spread it with butter and honey from the kitchen table. Automatically she wiped away the crumbs on the table top and shook the cloth over the sink. Finally, folding the bread and honey into a sandwich, she walked out of the kitchen into the passage.

The back door was open and warm air wafted in, fragrant with the country. She leaned against the frame, looking out. Half the yard was in deep shadow, the other half in bright sunlight. Immediately opposite her across the flagged court, the archway through the stable block was a dark tunnel with a view of the side drive disappearing round a bend and beyond the steep, wooded valley rising up out of sight behind the stable roof and then reappearing as an undulating line of green trees edging the blue and white sky.

Emma sighed. The fineness of the weather and the brilliance of the day only emphasized her own dejected spirits. They seemed to mock her like the voice in her head mocked her. 'Go on, Em! Go out and enjoy yourself. It'll do you good. Stuck inside all day!' it whispered, mimicking her mother and her grandmother and all the other people who always thought they knew what would be best for her.

Shaking her head, she put the last of the bread into her mouth and, after licking honey off her fingers, she turned her back on the outside world and retraced her steps along the corridor. When the voice in her head started talking it could go on for hours. However, over the years Emma had learned the best way to deal with it was to ignore it. She decided to wash her hair. It needed doing, it'd fill in time, but the real reason was that it would help her to ignore the voice.

As she ran up the stairs she could hear the builders banging away at the other end of the house. Reaching the end of the passage, she noticed her mother's door was open. The room was chaotic. Harriet hadn't unpacked her case but she'd obviously searched through it, probably looking for some missing article of clothing. Garments were strewn across the floor and on the bed. One of a pair of shoes was on the dressing table, the other one was nowhere to be seen. There was a half-empty mug of coffee with a lipstick lying beside it. A cigarette had been left to smoulder on the upturned lid of a make-up jar, leaving a trail of white ash protruding from its end. One bed was unmade, the other was covered with the contents from a portfolio that lay open on it. Papers and drawings were strewn in all directions with paint colour charts and fragments of material scattered haphazardly amongst them.

'Oh, God! Mother!' Emma groaned disgustedly and turning her back on the mess she slammed the door behind her.

The sound echoed down the corridor . . . *bang, bang, bang* . . . fading into the distance, an odd effect. Emma paused, looking back towards the stairs.

'Hello?' she called, wanting to hear the echo of her voice. But no sound came back to her. She reopened her mother's door and slammed it again. Silence; thick and airless like a blanket smothering her. No echo. She frowned thoughtfully and then shrugged. She must have imagined it.

Her own room was neat and uncluttered. She had unpacked after supper on the evening before and all her clothes were in the appropriate drawers and on the right hangers. She had made the bed and smoothed the bedspread. Even the curtains at the window were arranged and equally spaced. Her mother sometimes mocked Emma, like her voice mocked her, for her excessive tidiness. But what Harriet didn't understand was that the muddle in which she so happily lived was actually painful to her daughter. Untidiness could give Emma a headache. Worse, it made her feel dizzy and apprehensive. Although she could quite easily go around looking scruffy and had very little personal vanity, her surroundings had to be calm and ordered. If the room she was in was in a muddle she was afraid that the muddle would, somehow, get inside her mind. And when her mind was untidy the voice gained control. 'Emmy's tidying up,' it would chant. 'You're so fussy, Emmy, such a pain, Emmy. Boring Emmy, always neat and tidy.'

Now, determined not to let the voice start again, she hurried to collect her sponge bag from its place on the dressing table. Reaching the table she paused, looking at her reflection in the mirror. She pulled the neck of her T-shirt down, revealing the tattoo on her shoulder. The skin was still red and one of the needle marks was oozing and watery. She pressed at it gently to see if there was any actual pus, but none came out. The place was tender though and she peered at it, looking for signs of poisoning or infection.

Thus preoccupied and with her back to the room she felt suddenly as though someone was standing near her. It wasn't that she actually heard anything or saw anything, it was more the sensation of being watched – that enquiring glance from strangers as you first walk into a room that makes you uncomfortable and nervous and clumsy in your movements. She glanced up from the tattoo and looked in the mirror at the reflection of the room behind her. There was no one there. But a moment later a strange little sound, an unfamiliar *click*, made her swing round, immediately on her guard. At first she could see no indication of what could have caused the noise but, as she was searching, the

38

second doorway – the one that Lynda Carver had told her gave access to a staircase to the floor below – slowly swung open, creaking on its hinges.

Emma shivered as a sudden cold breeze blew through the room.

'Who's there?' she called. No answer came back to her. 'I know you're there. What d'you want? This is a private room you know.'

'Talking to yourself, Emmy!' her voice whispered in her head and she heard again the high fluting laughter that had accompanied her to sleep the night before. Only this time, although she still wanted to convince herself that she was only imagining the sound, it seemed to come from beyond the half-open doorway.

'If you think you can scare me,' Emma said, without being sure who she thought she was speaking to, 'you'll be sorry.' And to prove her courage, to herself as much as anyone else, she made a sudden dart for the door and pulled it fully open.

But no one was standing on the other side. The space beyond, no bigger than a large cupboard, was empty. As she stepped into it she saw a steep flight of steps disappearing down into the dark. The sound of the workmen hammering below was louder here. Emma could hear someone whistling and the mutter of conversation followed by laughter.

'They're all laughing at you, Em,' the voice whispered. 'Everyone's laughing.'

Emma shook her head and applied her mind instead to working out what could have happened. It was obvious that one of the builders had come up the stairs, opened the door, and then, seeing her in the room, had gone down again. Maybe whoever it was had meant to frighten her. It was one of those typical, stupid games that boys play. The best thing to do, she told herself, would be to ignore it; to go back into her room, shut and lock the door again and get on with washing her hair. . . .

Then a sudden memory made her gasp. The evening before, when she had tried it, the door wouldn't open. Lynda Carver had told her that it was always locked and that the key was kept on the bedroom side. It was still there, sticking out of the keyhole.

'How pathetic!' she said out loud, getting angry. 'Haven't you anything better to do? It's obvious how you did it. You came into my room earlier and unlocked the door. The cheek of it! This is a private room, you know.'

'Go on, Em! You tell them!' her voice encouraged her.

'You think I'm scared?' Emma said and she started to go down the steep stairs. But she'd only taken a couple of steps when the door above her slammed shut. Cutting out the light.

Her courage failed her at once. Absolute darkness surrounded her, thick and pressing. She started to struggle for air, her breathing getting faster and more shallow as fear and panic gripped her.

'Just calm down! Calm down, Emma!' she whispered. But even her own voice sounded muffled and unfamiliar. Turning round, she felt her way back up the steps. Like a blind person her fingers reached and groped until she found the knob. Turning it, she pushed at the door, but it wouldn't move.

The shock was so intense that Emma started to scream.

'Let me out,' she yelled, banging with her fists on the door. 'Please . . . someone . . . let me out!'

40

Now she was rattling the door knob, frantic to be out of the small dark space.

'Help me!' Emma screamed. 'Please ... somebody ... HELP ME!' and sinking onto her knees, she started to cry.

After a moment light appeared, glowing in from the bottom of the stairs, and a very human, matter-of-fact voice called out.

'You all right up there? Hello? I say ... anyone there?'

'Please,' Emma sobbed, 'get me out of here!'

Footsteps came quickly up the stairs behind her.

'What're you doing?' a friendly voice asked and, looking round, Emma could dimly make out Tom, the builder with the pony tail, peering at her through the half light.

'I'm locked in.' Emma wailed.

Tom leaned past her and turned the knob of the door. It swung open and sunlight from the bedroom flooded in around her.

'No, you're not!' Tom said, cheerfully.

Emma crawled forward into the room, shaking and gasping for air.

'Hey! You're really in a bad way,' Tom said, following her in and helping her to stand. 'How long have you been in there?'

'Not long,' Emma replied. 'I don't know how long. The door was locked, I couldn't get out.'

'Locked? No! I've just opened it, haven't I?'

'Don't worry, I'm all right now,' Emma told him, keeping her back to him, so that he couldn't see her tear-stained face.

'You're lucky I heard you,' Tom said, going back to the door. 'We're not working in the room down

41

there yet. I only came in to do some measuring. You're sure you're all right?'

'Yes, I'm fine. Just leave me alone,' Emma snapped, feeling suddenly angry.

'Maybe the latch stuck,' he said kindly, ignoring her tone and trying the handle a few times. 'I'll give it some oil when I've got a minute.' Then he disappeared down the stairs again.

'You must think I'm really stupid,' Emma shouted after him. 'I know it was one of you lot playing a pathetic joke.' She slammed the door closed and locked it. Then, gasping for air, she moved quickly to the window and leaned out.

2

Later, when she had calmed down, Emma went to the bathroom and washed her hair, kneeling on the ground by the bath and using the hand shower – which ran either furiously cold or trickled scalding water and refused to mix the two. Towelling her hair as she came back out, she almost collided with Lynda Carver leaving Harriet's room and obviously embarrassed at being caught.

'I thought you had gone with your mother,' she said, covering her confusion by attacking Emma.

'I've been washing my hair,' Emma replied, stating the obvious in a superior tone, expecting another cross-examination. But Lynda Carver hurried away along the corridor as though guilty of some crime and consequently not anxious to continue the conversation.

'Were you looking for something?' Emma called after her, enjoying having the upper hand.

'No,' the other woman replied, without turning.

'Then what were you doing in Mum's room?'

'I've been . . . collecting curtains for the cleaners,' Lynda replied, stopping and turning, obviously snatching at any story to explain her presence and defying Emma to question her further.

Emma stared pointedly at Lynda's empty hands.

'Curtains?'

'I've . . . decided I can have yours done after you've gone.'

They stared at each other with open animosity then Emma looked towards her room.

'Mrs Carver!' she called over her shoulder.

'Now what?'

'Can you come a minute?' and, as she spoke, she went into the room.

'I've got work to do,' Lynda Carver snapped. 'I can't spend the day lounging about, even if you can.' But Emma heard her footsteps coming slowly back along the corridor as she spoke. 'You're a nuisance, you are,' she said reaching the open door. 'You want to get yourself outside. A bit of fresh air would do you all the good in the world. . . .'

'Did you unlock this door?' Emma interrupted her, pointing towards the staircase door.

'Did I . . . what? No, I did not!' Lynda replied, sounding cross. 'And no more must you. I told you last night. Nasty steep stairs – there'll only be an accident if you go using them.' She seemed strangely on edge and angry.

'Well somebody did,' Emma said, resenting her tone.

'What are you talking about?'

'The door swung open . . .'

'When?'

43

'Just now – and when I went inside it shut behind me and I was locked in.'

For a moment Lynda Carver's face registered surprise and perhaps also fear then, with a shake of the head, she rounded on Emma.

'You want to watch it, young lady,' she said, spitting the words. 'You know what happened to the little boy who cried wolf . . . Keep telling lies and people won't believe you when you're telling the truth.'

'I'm not lying.'

'That door is kept locked – and if anyone opened it it must have been you.' She turned and disappeared back along the corridor.

'You still haven't said why you were poking about in Mother's room,' Emma yelled after her.

'Poking about? One more word out of you and I'll speak to your mother about you. . . .'

'Don't you worry, I'll be speaking to her first. She won't like to know you've been going through her things.'

Lynda Carver turned, her whole body shaking with anger.

'It isn't her room. It isn't a private room. It's a guest room. I am the housekeeper here – I have the right to go into any room I like,' she shouted.

'I didn't say you didn't have, did I?'

'Good gracious me! I go into Lady Shawcross's room all the time. I don't have to get her permission so I certainly don't need to ask the likes of you. . . .'

Lynda Carver had now reached the end of the landing and with a snort of disgust she disappeared down the stairs, muttering to herself and without giving a backward glance. Emma stuck out her tongue defiantly and went into her room, kicking

44

the door closed behind her. It slammed with a loud bang that seemed to echo through the house – *bang, bang bang, bang* – fading into silence.

The depression that she had felt earlier settled over her once more. After all the shouting and the sudden noise of the door slamming, the room seemed oppressively still and quiet. Drying her hair, she crossed to the dressing table. She sat on the stool and stared at herself in the mirror. The row had left her tense and shaken. She hadn't meant to lose her temper. She hadn't even meant to provoke Lynda. It had just happened. Now, sitting in the silent room, with the brilliant sunny morning beyond the window and surrounded by the stillness, she felt unreal and detached, as though she were an actor who had strayed into the wrong scene and, having no lines or part to play, was waiting for the next thing to happen and, until it did, was incapable of any action or even of coherent thought.

It was while she was in this negative, unformed state – half in and half out of the world, as it were – that she first heard the whispering. It was nothing very dramatic or spectacular at first. Perhaps if she had been busy or if her mind had been occupied with some thought it would have gone unnoticed. It must have been going on for some time before she became aware of it. It was so quiet that she could easily have missed it. But it was definitely there – a whispered conversation going on somewhere close to her. It wasn't as far away as the corridor, nor was it beyond the door to the nursery stairs. It was in the room with her. But when she looked round there was no one there. Nor could she pinpoint the precise position of the sound. Wherever she looked, the whispering seemed to be behind her.

45

She started turning and turning on the stool, looking quickly from left to right, suddenly swinging round, trying to locate the sound, to catch it unawares.

This jerky, agitated action seemed to amuse the whisperers. The muffled words became interspersed with trills of high, light, giggling laughter.

Eventually Emma stopped moving and tried to take control of herself. She took several deep slow breaths and folded her arms tightly across her chest, forcing herself to stop shaking. Then she listened again. The constant flow of buzzing, chattering whispers and giggling laughter continued behind her . . . but now, gradually, one word was separating out from the indistinguishable mass and she was able at last to give it some meaning.

A terrible panic gripped her. This new sound she could hear was her own name being whispered over and over again, as though she were being watched and maliciously talked about.

'Emma! Emma! E . . . mm . . . a!'

Emma started to shake. The fear she had been fighting broke loose, gripping at her throat and stomach. She covered her ears with her hands to block out the sound, and leaned against the dressing table as her head began to swim and she thought she was about to faint.

'Emma,' the voices whispered backwards and forwards, like an echo. 'Emma! Emma! Emma!' The tone had a greedy ring to it. It licked around her like a cat licks at cream. It savoured the sound of her name and it purred with delight. 'Emma!' it sighed on a exhalation of breath. 'Emma!' it crooned.

Finally Emma could bear the tension no longer.

She rose quickly and throwing her towel onto the bed, she grabbed a shirt and pulled it on, stuffing it into the belt of her jeans as she made for the door.

As she ran along the corridor she could still hear the sounds coming from her room. But now there was only the laughter; high, uncontrolled, delighted, childish laughter. The sort of laughter that seldom happens. The sort of laughter where you fall on your back, weak with glee, and shake with hysteria until it hurts and tears are streaming down your cheeks.

Emma went down the stairs three at a time and didn't stop running until she was out of the back door, across the yard and beyond the arch on the side drive in the bright, fresh air of the sparkling morning.

'What's happening to me?' she said out loud.

3

That evening Harriet suggested that after supper they should go to the local pub and 'check out the talent'.

'Mother!' Emma protested.

'What?'

'I can't stand it when you try to act young.'

'Hey! D'you mind!'

' "Check out the talent!" You sound like a granny on speed!'

Harriet sighed. She explained that she had had a long day. The woman in Helmsley was way behind with the curtains she was making and, when she'd returned to the house it was to discover from Tom that the walls behind the panelling they'd already removed were in bad shape and would need replastering before they were ready for painting. . . .

They were sitting in the kitchen having a mug of tea and it was the first time they'd seen each other all day. Harriet seemed on edge and was talking too fast.

'Replastering!' she groaned. 'That means I'll have to wait for it to dry out before I start doing the walls.'

'Is this your way of telling me we're going to have to stay here longer than planned?' Emma demanded.

'No. It just means I'll have to jig things round. I may have to come back later, on my own.' Harriet groaned. 'You'll have to stay with Muti – if she'll have you. Oh, hell!' But although her words were calculated to sound angry her mood was actually distracted and her eyes had a far-off look.

'Where were you all morning, anyway?' Emma asked, cutting herself a second piece of the shop-bought Battenburg cake Harriet had brought back with her.

'I told you – seeing the woman in Helmsley.'

'All morning?'

'What've you been doing?' Harriet asked, changing the subject. 'Had a good day?'

Emma shrugged. For a moment she was tempted to tell Harriet all that had happened but it quickly passed. After all, what would be the point? Harriet would hardly be likely to believe her, no halfway sane person would.

'I washed my hair and went for a walk,' she said instead. 'When you didn't come back at lunchtime I had a sandwich and went for another walk.'

'Yes. Sorry!' Harriet was flustered by this dig. 'I

48

should have phoned you to say I'd be late but . . .
I hadn't taken the phone number with me.'

Emma frowned. 'You mean you went out without
the Filofax?' she mocked. 'You must have felt
naked, Mother dear!' And, getting up, she crossed
to the door.

'Where are you going?'

'Watch telly.'

'I thought we were going out.'

'Where?'

'To the pub.'

'The pub?! Yuk! No thanks.'

'I thought it was decided,' Harriet protested.

'You may have decided, I certainly didn't,'
Emma replied.

'What's wrong with going to the pub? Oh, come
on, Em. Please.'

'Boring, Mother! Terribly, terribly boring,'
Emma called as she went through the house to the
little sitting room and switched on the TV.

'Not as boring as sitting inside watching telly,'
Harriet said, following her. 'Oh, come on, Em. I'll
go mad if I stay in all night.'

'You go if you want to.'

'I can't go out and leave you on your own.'

'I'm not going. I'm under age,' Emma said,
switching on the television.

'They don't worry about that in the country.'

'No, Mother.'

A moody silence settled around them.

In fact the last thing Emma wanted to was be
left alone in the house. She still hadn't worked out
what had really happened in the bedroom and had
spent a lot of the day trying to rationalize it. There
had to be a reasonable explanation she told herself.

But it was hard to come up with one and at the back of her mind nagged the growing fear that if she couldn't find a satisfactory answer then the only other possibility was that the voices were . . . not quite of this world. But what did that mean? That she was being haunted? How could that be? She didn't believe in ghosts . . .

Emma shook her head, banishing the jumble of thoughts and tried to concentrate on the television.

'Actually . . .' Harriet said, breaking the silence, 'd'you remember that chap, Simon Wentworth?'

'Who?'

'Simon Wentworth – I did some work for him last year. House in Islington? You must remember. He writes travel books. He was the one who got us tickets for the Bolshoi *Spartacus*. . . .'

'What about him?' Emma felt the stirrings of suspicion.

'I bumped into him!'

'Where?'

'Up here. Today. In a pub in Helmsley . . .'

'What were you doing in a pub?'

'Oh, do concentrate, darling.'

'I am doing. I am.'

'I took the curtain woman for lunch. I told you.'

'No you didn't.'

'Anyway,' Harriet persevered. 'There was Simon. I couldn't believe it!'

Emma stared at her mother thoughtfully.

'I bet you couldn't.'

Harriet moved away, unable to hold Emma's questioning eyes.

'He's up here doing some research,' she said, making it sound like a lame excuse.

'For?'

Harriet shrugged. 'A book he's writing, I suppose. He's staying in Helmsley . . .' again that apologetic, conspiratorial tone.

'And you want to have a drink with him.'

'I want US to have a drink with him.'

Emma continued her long, cool stare, enjoying watching Harriet squirm then, with a little satisfied smile, she turned and flicked channels on the television set.

'You don't need me along, Mother dear!' she said.

Harriet hesitated for a moment then decided not to continue the conversation.

'I'm going to have a gin. D'you want anything?' she asked innocently going to the door.

'No thanks,' Emma called, staring at the set without really seeing the picture. 'Don't have too much. You'll be driving later.'

Harriet returned, glass in hand, in time for The Six O'Clock News. It had just started when the phone rang. Emma, who was nearest, answered it.

Her grandmother's voice:

'Did you all die, or something?'

'Hi, Muti!' Emma said, pleased it was her.

'Don't you Muti me! How dare you both go off without so much as a word?'

'Mum came to see you.'

'When?'

'The night before last.'

'Balls! I haven't seen her for so long I can't remember what she looks like.' Laura Charrington's voice crackled down the line. 'I've been abandoned by you both. I feel like a discarded rag.'

'Muti!' Emma protested, trying to cut across the tirade. 'What on earth does a rag feel like?'

51

'Like I do,' her grandmother replied, crisply. 'I've been ringing the Putney house so much I've broken the nail on my index finger. Then I remembered that you were away. . . .'

'I'll put you on to Mum,' Emma said.

'Don't you dare. I never want to speak to her again . . .'

Emma passed the phone to Harriet.

'It's Muti. She's in one of her moods.'

'Hello, Mother!' Harriet said in an overly patient tone and then, turning her back on Emma, she leaned against the back of the sofa and spoke quietly into the phone, adopting her smooth, reasonable, have-we-a-problem-here? voice.

Emma's attention was half on the television and half on the conversation behind her – neither was making much sense. What little she could hear of what Harriet was saying suggested that Laura felt she'd been let down in some way. Harriet protested a lot, but in an unnaturally quiet voice – as though she didn't want Emma to hear. At one moment she almost lost her temper. 'We've been through all this, Mother!' she snapped. Later she became more conciliatory again. 'I'm sorry if there's been some confusion,' she said – and she glanced at Emma, who by this time was openly staring, and raised her eyebrows. 'Yes, Mother. I promise. We'll phone you later in the week. Bye now . . .' and she replaced the receiver.

'What was all that about?' Emma asked.

Harriet shook her head and looked irritated. 'Her brain is going. Senile dementia.'

'That's not a very nice thing to say about your own mother.'

'We must face up to it.'

52

'Muti? Don't be silly. She's brighter than both of us. What was she saying?'

'Nothing in the least important.'

'Didn't you go and see her the other night?'

'Of course I did.' Harriet replied, rising. 'I'll go and make supper.'

'Mother,' Emma said, still staring at the television set and stopping Harriet before she'd reached the door.

'What?'

'You're a very bad liar. Did you know that?'

Harriet turned and looked at her.

'Don't you start, Em!' she said, her voice full of suppressed anger. 'I warn you. Just . . . leave me alone.' And she turned and slammed out of the room.

'Oops!' the voice whispered in her head. 'Well done, Emmy dear. You handled that one really well, didn't you?'

DIARY

Why does Mother find it necessary to lie every time she starts an affair? I always know it's happening, so it really is pointless. On the other hand – why does mother bother to have affairs? They've never come to anything. At least my father goes in for a bit of glamour and does it all (and I do mean ALL) with a certain amount of style. But Mother . . . ! Simon Wentworth! The name sounds like a character out of a sitcom. He is so yukky. So smooth. All that crap he talked about being an explorer. I bet he's never set foot on foreign soil without a first class return ticket and a wad of cash from his publisher in his back pocket. Even I could be an 'explorer' if someone else was paying for it. She can't be serious. But of course she will be. Simon Wentworth is just the sort of nerd Mother would fall for. Well I shall let her know exactly what I think of him. I do not intend to have Simon Wentworth as a stepfather. Muti will go ape. She and I have exactly the same views about Mother's men. She once said 'Harriet's taste in men is much the same as Dracula's taste in women used to be – absolutely bloody!' Darling Muti! I wish she was here – at least we could have a laugh. If Mother's so keen on having sex – why didn't she stay with Father? She'd already got the pick of the bunch and we could all have been rich and glitzy together. I would now be one of the brat pack appearing in movies and Hello *magazine. Why did she have to go and divorce him? I've never understood what went wrong and when I ask I only get a pained expression and am told to mind my own business. But it is my business. Muti is no help either. She just shrugs and looks mysterious and says it was all a long time ago and I needn't bother about it. It's almost as though they think it was my fault that Mum and Father split up. I expect I was an unwanted pregnancy. Well, I can't be blamed for THAT. It isn't very nice going through life knowing you're 'unwanted'. They should be doubly kind to me. Instead of which Mother is a pain and Father ignores me. This is a long entry because I'm alone in the house and I wanted someone to talk to. She never thinks about that – that I might be lonely. Tonight's typical. She's gone off to meet the dreaded Wentworth and although she pretended to want me to go with her . . . it was obvious that I'd only*

Three

1

Emma stopped writing in mid-sentence and turned her head. A distant sound had interrupted her train of thought but now as she held her breath and listened there was only the silence, dull and throbbing, spreading away from her to every corner of the vast house and out into the isolated country that surrounded it.

This is the quietest place I've ever been in, she thought, and the loneliest. I feel as if I'm the only living person in the world. Putting down the notebook she was using as a diary, she crossed to the window and leaned against the frame, staring out. Through the gathering dusk she could see the paved courtyard and the front of the house stretching to the centre porch and on to where the other wing jutted towards the ornate railings and gates.

'I shall go mad with boredom here,' she said out loud, her voice scarcely penetrating the silence. 'In fact I probably am already mad and that's why I'm talking to myself.' She shook her head. The view from the window only added to her depression, with its emptiness and complete lack of sound. She found herself longing for busy streets full of people and exhaust fumes and the noise of traffic.

'Oh, I wish I was at home!' she sighed, suddenly fighting back tears.

'I wish I was at home!' her head-voice mimicked in a sing-song tone. 'Poor Emmy! Don't cry!' and then it laughed, a high thin giggle.

'Shut up!' Emma snapped and she kicked the wall beneath the window as though she blamed the house for her mood.

'Oops! Temper!' the voice sang.

Emma turned her back on the view irritably and was about to return to the settee, when a glint of flashing light caught her attention. Looking back quickly her eyes were dazzled by a bright gleam piercing the gloom outside the window. Holding up her hand to prevent being blinded, she peered through her spread fingers. The light was coming from one of the side windows on the first floor of the distant wing. She was almost certain that it was the same window in which she had seen a light the evening that they'd arrived.

It must be a broken pane or something, she decided, catching the last of the sun, and she was returning to the settee when a new thought made her stomach lurch. The sun couldn't possibly be shining on that side of the house. It faced east and would get the morning light. Besides, the sun had long gone. It was nearly dark. She turned slowly. Even as she watched, the view outside was blurring into dusk and shadow. She peered at the distant window. Again, after a moment, the flashing light appeared, dazzling her eyes. It was as though the beam was being aimed at her – like a child would play with a mirror. Emma moved and the light

56

moved with her. She ducked out of sight and then, within moments of her returning to the window, the light sought out and found her eyes again.

There's somebody up there, she thought and at once, as if in confirmation of the idea, she heard the noise that had disturbed her earlier. It was the sound of footsteps, pounding above her – the heavy thump of feet, moving quickly, as though a race were being run along an upstairs corridor in the main part of the house – the part into which she had not so far ventured.

Emma went quickly out of the room. The little sitting room was situated in the front wing at the kitchen end of the house. A short corridor led from it to double doors which connected with the rest of the house. She crossed and pushed them open.

The hall she entered was filled with gloom and shadows. Only a glimmer of last light came through the window above the entrance doors as the dusk finally faded into night.

Emma listened again. The house was silent and still. Dimly she could make out the staircase rising from the centre of the hall and then dividing into two flights that struck off in opposite directions, reaching the galleried landing at facing corners. She felt along the wall beside her, searching for a light switch. Finding none, she tiptoed over to the main entrance and located two rows of switches on a brass plate set into the wall. She flicked one and a lantern in the porch sprang into light, casting strange elongated shadows back into the hall through the windows of the inner doors. She flicked the switch up again and the light went out. She tried a lower switch and light glimmered from an unseen source along one of the corridors that disappeared from the corners of the upper gallery. She pressed the switch beside it and the opposite corridor was similarly illuminated. The light spill lessened the darkness in the hall a little and drew Emma's interest and attention towards the staircase. She crossed and was actually starting to climb the steps before she thought that it would be much more sensible and reassuring to put on the hall's main light first.

'Stupid,' she whispered and went back to the switches.

'What goes up, must come down!' her head-voice murmured.

'Oh, how very wise!' Emma taunted herself and she pressed her finger on the other top switch beside the one that served the porch light.

The hall flooded with light as the chandelier hanging from the centre of the ceiling lit up.

'What goes up, must come down!' the voice sang.

'Oh, shut up!' Emma said, the light giving her confidence, and she crossed to the stairs and started to go up two at a time, as though she knew that if she went slowly her courage would fail her.

'What goes up, must come down!' the voice said for a third time. Only now it sounded much louder. Now it was almost as if it wasn't in Emma's head at all but had somehow become free and was taunting her from a distance.

'That's a really stupid thing to keep saying,' Emma shouted, turning her face upwards in the direction from which the voice seemed to be coming. 'It's completely meaningless!'

She had reached the half-landing, where the stairs divided. She paused, unsure which route to take. Her breathing was shallow and rapid and she

58

could feel her heart beating too fast as the fear she was trying to suppress struggled to overwhelm her.

'What goes up, must come down!' the voice crooned with a satisfied tone, then it giggled playfully. 'What goes on . . . can also go off!'

The chandelier went out, plunging the hall into instant darkness.

Emma screamed. Her whole body started to shake. The lights in both the upper corridors were still on and the childish giggling seemed to come from somewhere up there. For a moment she was rooted to the spot, unable to move as fear and panic gripped her body, making her gasp and fight for breath. She turned slowly, looking up at the chandelier. How could it have gone off unless it had been switched off? And, if it had been switched off – by whom?

'Who's there?' she shouted and she made a move to go back down to the hall when behind and above her, up on the landing, the noise of running footsteps made her spin round.

'Who are you?' she shouted. 'What d'you want?' Sudden, fierce anger swept over her. 'I know you're there,' she yelled and she raced up the stairs two at a time in pursuit of the sound.

Reaching the galleried landing, she paused again. The silence had returned, stifling and thick around her. Then, a moment later, a door banged – a sharp, sudden sound – making her jump. The noise had come from the corridor which led to the opposite part of the house from the kitchen quarters and the little sitting room where she had so recently been sitting writing her diary. For a moment Emma was tempted to hurry back down the stairs and return to its safety. But she had to find out what was going on. There had to be an explanation. So, taking a deep breath to make herself brave, she started to walk along the corridor in the direction from which the sound had come.

There were three doors on each side of the passage, all of them closed, and at the end a window with curtains hanging open revealing the blank, dark night outside.

The silence was everywhere.

This is silly, she thought, slowing to a standstill as her courage wavered. I may as well go back to the sitting room. If I want to explore I can do it much better in daylight ... and she turned to retrace her steps.

BANG!

Ahead of her one of the doors, closer to the galleried landing, slammed. She actually saw it open and close before she wheeled away and ran, gasping, towards the end of the passage.

A face, with staring eyes, white-skinned and ghost-like, leapt at her out of the darkness, making her sob and cry out, screwing up her eyes with terror.

'What is it?' she screamed. 'What's happening to me?' The face in front of her mimicked her every move, her every expression.

'What's happening to me? What's happening to me?' a voice whispered, somewhere near her shoulder.

Slowly Emma sank down onto her knees in front of the landing window, her hands covering her ears to block out the sound. As she did so the ghost face moved with her, covering its ears, as if in a mirror. . . .

Emma stared at the face and through it at the

dark night outside. Then she smiled. The ghost face smiled back. Emma took her hands from her ears, the ghost hands followed suit. She waved, the ghost waved. She stuck out her tongue and so did the ghost.

'Steady, Em!' she gasped, and she started to laugh. 'It's only my reflection! I really must get a hold on myself. It's my reflection in the glass . . .' and leaning against the sill, she pressed her forehead against the forehead of the ghost and felt the cool of the window pane on her brow.

'Honestly!' she whispered. 'What is the matter with me?'

Rising unsteadily, she went through the open door into the room on her left and felt along the wall for a light switch.

She was in one of the rooms that the builders had been working on. There was a pile of panelling heaped in the centre of the floor from the walls that had already been stripped and everywhere there was dust, the air was thick with it.

The room was long and narrow with, at its far end, windows on three sides. Emma realized that she was in the opposite wing to the one in which the little sitting room was situated. But where that wing had a number of smaller rooms in it, here the whole area was given over to one large space. It was from one of these windows that she had seen the light flashing. She crossed to a window and looked out into the dark, then she turned and surveyed the room. It was surprisingly drab and ordinary. The centre light was without a shade and cast harsh shadows. Emma felt her depression returning. She wandered round the room, looking out of the curtainless windows at the wall of night.

'Em?' a voice called, distantly. 'Are you there?'

For a moment she felt the prickle of fear again at the nape of her neck. But she crossed quickly to the door, calling.

'I'm here!'

'I saw the lights on, I thought we had a burglar,' her mother said, coming into the room. 'You all right?'

'Fine!'

Both their voices were too bright; unreal, hiding deeper, more complicated emotions.

'I hoped they'd have done more than this,' Harriet said, walking round the room. 'You must admit it's going to be better without this awful panelling.' She crossed to one of the windows and inspected the window frame carefully. 'You should have come out with us,' she continued, with her back now turned towards Emma. 'Simon was disappointed.'

'Simon?' Emma exclaimed. 'He hardly knows me.'

Harriet shrugged. 'I think he felt guilty about taking me away and leaving you all on your own.'

'I didn't mind.'

'What have you done?'

'I read a bit,' Emma mumbled.

'You should have come out. You've been stuck inside all day.'

'I didn't want to,' Emma said, feeling irritation growing.

'Please yourself,' Harriet said with a sigh. Seeing something that caught her attention on the floor, she bent to pick it up, saying in a nonchalant way as she did so. 'Simon wants to take us out to dinner. I said I'd ask you.'

Emma shrugged. 'I'm sure you'd much rather go on your own,' she said.

'Look at this!' Harriet exclaimed, ignoring Emma and staring thoughtfully at the object in her hand.

'No, you look at it, Mother. You obviously couldn't care less whether I do or not,' Emma snapped, feeling her mother's lack of interest in her as a further rejection.

Harriet glanced up, surprised by her tone. As she did so, Emma caught sight of the thing she was holding. 'What is it anyway?' she asked with bad grace, not wanting to admit interest but unable to take her eyes off the object.

'A lorgnette,' her mother replied, holding up the tiny pair of spectacles by their handle so that Emma could see them. 'I wonder where they came from. They look quite old. D'you suppose they could have been behind the panelling?'

As Harriet studied the lorgnette, the glass reflected the light from the naked bulb in the centre of the ceiling, dazzling Emma momentarily.

She lifted her hand, warding off the bright ray, and backed away towards the door.

'Sorry!' Harriet said, with a smile. 'Was I blinding you?'

'I'm going back downstairs,' Emma said and she went quickly out of the room, without giving her mother a second look.

As she turned into the corridor the door opposite clicked shut. She heard the sound, but she didn't stop to investigate.

I've had enough for one night, she thought and she hurried away towards the stairs.

The woman in the long dress seemed agitated. She lifted the cushions, one by one, and looked behind them. She pushed her hand down the gap between the deeply padded back and the seat and felt all the way along. She lowered herself onto her knees and reached under the sofa, her hand searching the carpet, like a blind person seeing by touch. Then, failing to find whatever it was she had obviously lost, she rose once more and sat on the edge of the sofa, scanning the room with myopic eyes. The room was long, with a number of windows on the three sides of its farther end, each of them draped with curtains of looped and gathered fabric decorated with stripes of gold, silver and black. There were a number of sofas along the walls at the door end, with pictures of hunting scenes hanging above them on the plain white walls. A fire was burning in the hearth, with an ornate mirror over the mantle. A billiard table occupied the centre of the room. The woman rose and wandered in a distracted fashion, searching the floor with her eyes. Reaching the table, she leaned against it, a weary and bewildered expression on her face. Then something made her look up quickly. She brushed stray hair from her forehead, a quick, nervous gesture. Her expression changed from agitation to one of fear. She could hear giggling. At first it was distant and light, like the ripple of water, but as it grew in volume it became ominous and excluding – the sound of a joke that you are not invited to share, a joke against yourself. The woman turned in the direction of the sound. As she did so the scene exploded into brilliant light, dazzling the eyes, impossible to watch without being blinded. The giggling grew louder and more hysterical.

Emma woke with a start.

Total darkness surrounded her. The dream had vanished. But for a moment, the giggling remained – breathless and exaggerated, humourless and cruel.

Emma reached out and felt for the bedside lamp. The pink and white room snapped into view. With it came silence, punctuated by the distant screech of an owl.

Emma pulled the covers closely round her shoulders and hugged herself. One hand brushed the area of her tattoo. The flesh was hot and sore to touch. She felt suddenly sick and her head ached.

The ink's probably poisoned me, she thought. I shall die a horrible death. Taken in her youth by a poisoned tattoo, they'll say.

Then she remembered her dream.

DIARY

The room was the one I was in last night – the one the builders are working on. And the woman was looking for her glasses. You could tell she had bad eyes by the way she stared. She was looking for her glasses – the ones Mother found. It all fits perfectly. Then she heard giggling and, next, whoever stole the glasses (kids – obviously) used them to dazzle her. It was a really classic dream – triggered by what had just happened to me. The room wasn't exactly the same. The panelling had gone. Maybe I was dreaming some time before it had been put up. (That would explain the woman's old-fashioned dress.) It was a Games Room. There was a snooker table in the middle. Snooker?? Don't know. Surely snooker started much later in The States in smoky dives – or is that pool? Is there a difference?

Find out when snooker was first played. BILLIARDS! Is there a difference? When was billiards first invented? Do you invent games???

THE WOMAN – who was she? She didn't look like a servant and yet she wasn't well dressed enough to be the mistress of a house like this. Her clothes were quite plain. She was scared – really scared – when the giggling started. (It's always kids by the sound. High and hysterical. It's the same when I hear it . . . or rather when I IMAGINE I do.) Maybe she was the babysitter! The NANNY. Yes – that's it. She was the nanny.

That means she used to sleep in this room. Lynda C. said this was the nanny's room. No, not nanny – GOVERNESS, that's what she said. 'This was always the governess room.' She was a governess. Yes, she had the look. Prim and proper – brainy. A spinster. Tight and precise. Just the sort of person young kids would pick on.

On the following page Emma drew a picture of the woman she had seen in her dream. She remembered the dress as well as she could. Long, with looped panels at the hips and caught up into folds at the back. Severely plain, in a dark material. The face long and sad looking. The hair, black.

Then she continued writing:

The woman had a fringe and her hair, rather like the skirt of the dress, was caught back off the head, with tight little curls. She had a pale face – no make-up. The hair was dark. She was obviously shortsighted. But, most important, she was scared. When she sat on the sofa – she sat right on the edge, as if she was ready to spring up the minute anyone came in. What was she scared of? Kids

66

playing a game? If they are kids. I mean, I'm only
guessing. Because of the laughter.

THE LAUGHTER – it wasn't friendly. It had . . .
a really cruel sound. As though, whoever it was, was
laughing at her.

Like they laugh at me. Who do? Why?
Mad, Emma. You're off the wall.

Four

1

The day was warm and overcast. Not a breath of air stirred in the valley. The trees round the pond stood motionless, heavy with summer leaf, trailing their branches on the surface of the water like tired hands dipping from the edge of a slowly drifting punt.

Emma lay on her back in the rough grass and stared up at the hazy clouds that covered the sky, turning it blank and colourless. She had brought with her a book and a sketch pad, pencils, a rubber, a couple of apples, a packet of biscuits, sun cream, her swimming things, a towel, and her diary. She'd loaded everything into a carrier bag and set out soon after breakfast. Harriet was in conference with the builders and Emma left without bothering to tell her she was going or where. Not that she knew herself. She hadn't made any specific plans. She just wanted to be out of the house and on her own. Most of all she wanted to be on her own.

As she was crossing the side yard she'd passed Lynda Carter arriving in her car. It was already after ten so Lynda was late and she glared at Emma defiantly, as if daring her to make some comment.

But Emma couldn't be bothered. She didn't even raise her hand in a wave. She just walked past the car as it pulled round to park in the yard and went through the arch onto the back drive without pausing.

Reaching the lane, she had walked along it until she'd reached the main gates with the long drive stretching up to the second set of gates with the house spread out behind them. Here she had sat for a while doing a sketch, but the view of the house was too distant to be of real interest and the oppressive atmosphere of the day made her head ache.

Eventually she'd abandoned the drawing and put the pad back into the carrier. She felt peculiarly exposed and vulnerable, sitting in the open at the end of the drive. She wanted shelter and obscurity. She decided to make her way to the pond that she had seen from her bedroom window on the other side of the house. Perhaps the intention to go there had always been in her mind – why else had she decided to bring her swimming costume and a towel? – but now she was attracted to it because she wanted the privacy of the trees and somewhere to hide from all the staring windows.

She rose quickly and crossed to climb over the iron fence that separated the drive from the meadow. Then she made her way through the lush grass, skirting the house at a distance, circling it like an animal watching its prey.

Or wasn't it really she who was the prey? That's how it felt. Every window watched her. The building itself seemed poised, as if ready to pounce.

At the other side of the house the meadow sloped away from the wrought iron railing that separated the formal lawns and terrace of the gardens from the park land. Emma could see her bedroom window set into the roof, the only one on that side of the house that was open. Again she experienced the uncomfortable feeling that she was being watched. She shaded her eyes against the hazy light and raked the rows of blank, staring windows, trying to catch a telltale movement that would reveal Lynda Carter or one of the builders looking out. But there was no sign of life in the house. It seemed as still and empty as a framed watercolour picture – and as unreal. Emma realized, suddenly, that that was part of its effect on her. The house was so far removed from anything in her knowledge that she couldn't connect with it. What had she, Emma Hartley, got to do with a big sprawling mansion in the middle of the country? Nothing. She was an outsider looking in at a strange, never experienced world. But when she was inside the house, looking out, was it any different then, she wondered? When she was part of the view, did she belong then? If a face looked out of one of those windows now and she recognized it as her own would she consider that she belonged there? Or would she still recognize herself as an outsider, a visitor, an immigrant?

'Too much thinking,' she told herself, speaking aloud. Her voice sounded muffled and unreal as if even it didn't belong to her.

So Emma had turned her back on the house and had hurried across the meadow until she was under the welcoming shelter of the trees.

Now, lying on her back and staring up through the branches at the blank sky, she realized that she'd been asleep. Her watch told her it was twenty past twelve. At first she was inclined to think it must be wrong, she couldn't believe that so much time had passed. Her book lay abandoned on the grass beside her. The carrier bag containing only her swimming things was under her head as a make-shift pillow, the rest of the contents were in a neat pile near by.

'I must have dropped off!' she said, her voice breaking the silence. Then she laughed and at once felt foolish.

'Talking to yourself again, Emmy dear!' her other voice whispered.

She sat up quickly and looked around her, not wanting the head-voice to start mocking. Gnats danced on the surface of the pond and a profound stillness hung on the air. The muggy heat was intense. Although she was only wearing a shirt, jeans and sandals Emma was sweating profusely. A sudden desire to get into the cool water of the pond overwhelmed her. There was no one anywhere near and so, slipping off her few clothes she didn't bother to put on her swimming costume before she gingerly crept into the water. The bottom of the pond was muddy and slimy to walk on but the water was so cool and soothing that it completely made up for any initial unpleasantness. Emma waded slowly away from the shore passing the long fronds of a willow that leaned over the bank to her left. When she was almost at the centre of the pond and still only waist deep in the water she turned slowly allowing her hands to brush the surface, sending tiny ripples fanning away from her, and looked back at the shore. The willow tree was immediately in front of her. To the left of it she could see her belongings lying on the shore. Splashing water, she turned and waded a few steps in the opposite direction. As she did so the shore to the right of the willow came more into view and there, staring at her, with a fishing rod in his hand, was a boy.

The look of stunned astonishment that his face registered when he saw her was only equalled by the gasp of surprise from Emma. She was standing waist deep in the pond, stark naked, and directly in his line of vision.

'Oh!' she yelled and as she did so she dropped down into the water until only her head and shoulders were above the surface.

For a moment they eyed each other in silence, then they both spoke at once.

'Go away!' Emma shouted.

'What are you doing here?' the boy gasped.

'I'm warning you – go on! Go away, pervert!' Emma shouted, embarrassment making her angry.

'I've got as much right to be here as you have.'

'Oh, I suppose you're one of the Shawcrosses, are you?' Emma spat, trying to sound sarcastic.

'No. And neither are you,' the boy replied.

'I'm a friend of the family,' Emma said. Her teeth were beginning to chatter because of the cold water.

'Well, that's funny, isn't it? Because the family are away.'

'They're letting me use the house – for a holiday.'

'Get away,' the boy said with a broad grin. 'I know exactly who you are.'

'Oh?'

'You're the daughter of the decorator woman they've got in.'

'You seem to know a lot that doesn't concern you.' Emma was trying so hard to sound superior and in control – but it wasn't easy while crouching

72

down in the cold water with her knees bent and her feet deep in the pond mud.

'Don't be stupid! The whole valley knows about you!' the boy said, then he cleared his throat and flicked his fishing line.

'Would you mind moving,' Emma said, trying to wither and sounding petulant instead. 'Go on! This water is freezing.'

'D'you want me to come in and fetch you?' he said casually, concentrating on spooling in the line.

'No!' Emma screamed.

The boy looked up and grinned at her.

'I can't move with you sitting there,' a note of pleading had crept into Emma's voice. 'I happen to have no clothes on.'

'Sorry! But you do look rather funny!' Then he laughed and turned his back. 'Go on, then! I won't look. I promise.'

Emma moved as fast as she could with her knees bent until the willow was between her and the boy. Then rising she splashed out of the pond and grabbed a towel.

'How long have you been there?' the boy called from the other side of the tree. 'I never saw you come.'

'Ages. And as I got here first I have prior claim – so you can go,' Emma replied, pulling her clothes over her damp, cold body.

'Ah, but I'm local – so I have more right.'

'But I'm not trespassing – and you are,' Emma called, feeling more secure as she zipped up her jeans.

'Point taken,' the boy called after a moment. 'Are you decent yet?'

'Yes!' Emma replied, feeling suddenly foolish again.

'Can I come round, then?' the boy called.

'If you must,' Emma replied.

She was sitting on the ground fastening her shoes when he appeared round the side of the willow. He wasn't carrying his fishing rod so he must have left his things where he'd been sitting. He was quite tall with short, dark hair that stuck up at the back. He was wearing loose baggy trousers and an open necked cream shirt.

'You gave me the shock of my life,' he said, coming into her view. 'I thought you were a ghost or something!'

'Not half as much of a shock as you gave me,' Emma replied. 'I was stark naked at the time!'

The boy grinned. 'It's all right. I didn't see any of the naughty bits. The first I knew was when you hit the water. I thought I'd landed a shark or something.'

'Are there really fish in there?' Emma asked, looking out at the pond.

'Yes!' the boy replied, sitting down beside her on the grass. 'Trout. Sir Michael's a great fisherman.'

'Oh, you know Sir Michael, do you? Emma asked, a mocking note creeping into her voice.

'No! I've seen him a few times – but I don't know him. They don't mix with the village. D'you want a mint?' and rummaging in his trouser pocket he produced a stick of Polos.

'Go on then,' Emma said, taking one.

They sucked in silence for a few moments. Emma felt increasingly breathless and shy. Eventually the boy glanced at her sideways and smiled.

'So anyway, I'm Tim.'

Emma giggled.

'What's so funny?' he asked, on the defensive.

'Tim? What a name! As in Tiny?' Emma spluttered with laughter again.

'No – as in Timothy, if you must know.'

'Timothy!'

'What's wrong with that?'

'It's an awful name.'

'Well, I didn't choose it, did I? I was given it. And I've learnt to live with it, so you can stop mocking. What's yours anyway?'

'Emma,' she said, then she held up a hand and sighed at the same time. 'I know. It's not much better. I think Mother was an Austen-freak at the time.'

'You mean she was into old cars?'

'No! Jane Austen! The author,' Emma replied, hoping she sounded withering. 'This is probably all a bit intellectual for you. You country folk don't have much time for literature, do you?'

'Jane Austen, 1775 to 1817. *Emma* is one of her last novels. . . . Though not actually *the* last. Because *Persuasion* comes after it. . . . D'you want more? English is my subject.'

'Amazing!' Emma said, feeling irritated.

They lapsed into silence again.

'She's nice looking,' Tim said after a while, in a voice that was trying to make amends. 'Your mother, I mean.'

'What a horribly sexist remark.'

'Why? If she is what's wrong with saying so?'

'You wouldn't have said it if she was a man.'

'Probably not. I just meant . . . she was nice looking.'

'How d'you know anyway?'

'I saw her last night in The Lion . . . the pub in the village. She was there with a man.'

'Oh! Shock! Horror!' Emma cried, throwing up her hands. 'I bet that set the village talking.'

'Certainly did,' Tim replied, then he grinned. 'She's supposed to be here on her own.'

'She's not on her own – I'm with her.'

'I meant without a man.'

'I see. I don't count because I'm a woman?'

'Oh, leave off!' Tim groaned.

'She's not up here with him, anyway,' Emma said too hurriedly and feeling colour rushing to her cheeks. 'He's just a friend whom she happened to bump into. He's doing research for a book. Mother's known him for ages. He's . . . a friend, that's all.'

'Well that's got that sorted out then!' Tim said, and he grinned again.

There was another awkward silence. Emma felt that somehow he was mocking her.

'What were you doing in a pub, anyway?' she demanded, allowing aggression to cover her confusion.

'Playing darts.'

'You're under age.'

'How d'you know?'

'I bet you're not eighteen.'

'All right, shop me to the fuzz!'

'The fuzz?! Honestly!'

The silence again. Emma plucked at the grass beside her, ripping it between her finger and thumb. The boy, Tim, picked up a small stone and threw it, skimming across the surface of the pond.

'Is that why you weren't there?' he asked, not looking at her.

'Where?' she said, surprised by the question.

'At the pub last night – with your mother and her boyfriend? Were you worried about being under age?'

'He's not her boyfriend,' Emma snapped, losing her temper. 'I've got better things to do with my time than sit in a pub,' and she shrugged and stretched, trying to appear nonchalant.

'I certainly wouldn't want to stay alone in that house,' Tim said and as he spoke he looked back over his shoulder. It was said in such a matter of fact voice but the words sent a shiver down Emma's spine.

'Why?' she asked, looking at him for the first time in ages.

'Have you met Mrs Carver's father?'

'Oh, of course I have! I pop round to tea every other day.'

'Sarcasm doesn't suit you.'

'Well, honestly! Why would I want to know Lynda Carver's father. She's bad enough – I don't want to meet any more of her ghastly family.'

'He's nice actually. I used to see him quite a bit. He used to do gardening for us until he got too old . . .'

'Why are we talking about him, anyway?'

'It's just – he once told me the place was haunted.'

'What place?' Emma asked, surprised by the suddenness of the statement.

'The Hall.'

'And you believed him . . . ?'

'Not now, no. But then I did. I was only about seven at the time. It gave me sleepless nights.'

'What did he actually say?'

'Just that – I mean he didn't go into details. . . .'

'Well, didn't you ask him?'

'No,' Tim said, with a dismissive grin.

'Why?' Emma could feel her frustration bubbling over. 'Honestly!'

'What?'

'Well, you're told something really important and you don't bother even to ask questions.'

'Like I say – I was only a kid. And now . . . well, I don't go in for all that supernatural rubbish.'

'You've just said you wouldn't like to spend time there alone.'

Tim turned once more to stare over his shoulder at the distant house that could be seen rising out of the dull haze that had settled over the valley.

'Yeah,' he said. 'I did, didn't I?' then he frowned. 'Don't know why really. Maybe it was what Mr Carver said all those years ago – but I always think the house looks sort of . . . unfriendly . . . Like as if it's in waiting.'

Emma stared at the house, but decided to say nothing.

'Actually I've never been inside,' Tim continued. 'So I don't really know what I'm talking about. I wouldn't mind seeing over the place sometime.'

'Be my guest,' Emma said in an absent voice.

'I thought you'd never ask!'

The uneasy silence settled over them once more. It seemed to match the oppressive atmosphere of the day. The hazy sunlight had completely gone now, obliterated by heavy rain clouds that were stealing in over the side of the valley behind the house. Emma's mind was teeming with so many half-formed questions and ideas that she was getting a headache.

'Feels like thunder,' Tim said, glancing at his watch. 'Hey, I'd better go! I'm off to Whitby this afternoon. D'you want to come?'

'No,' Emma replied, without really having heard his question.

'I'll see you then,' he said and getting up off the ground he turned towards the willow tree.

'No, don't go for a minute,' Emma said, breathlessly.

'I must – I've promised to change some library books for my Mum. If I don't go now, I'll miss the bus.'

Emma stared at him for a moment. She felt a sudden wave of spitefulness sweep over her.

'Oh, isn't that nice!' she mocked. The voice didn't sound like hers. It had the vicious, mocking tone of her head-voice. 'Proper little mother's boy, aren't you?'

Tim looked at her and for a moment it seemed as if he was going to say something but then thought better of it.

'Well, go on. Run and do as you're told!'

'Yeah, OK,' Tim said after a moment. 'I'll see you sometime, then,' and he walked away from her.

'Not if I see you first, you won't,' Emma's other voice called.

Tim stopped and looked back at her. 'There was a murder at Borthwick, you know.'

'At the house?' Emma gasped.

'Yeah.'

'Go on! You're just saying that to get my interest.'

'No, honestly. It's quite a famous case. Well, it is round here where nothing much happens. It was sometime during the last century, I think.'

'Who was murdered?'

79

'My mum knows all the details. She did some research. Something about a governess and a little boy found dead in . . . "peculiar circumstances". So, you see, maybe Mr Carver was right – watch out, there's a ghost about!' and turning once more he hurried round the hanging willow branches and disappeared.

2

Lynda Carver was sitting in the kitchen reading a newspaper when Emma came in. The Battenburg cake was in the middle of the table next to a teapot surrounded by empty mugs.

'If you want tea you'll have to make it yourself. The lads have had theirs with your mother. Where have you been anyway? She was looking for you.'

'Out,' Emma said with a shrug.

'Well, you should have said. She waited dinner for you until half past one.'

'We don't usually eat until the evening.'

'She'd made sandwiches specially.'

Emma stretched across the table and cut herself a piece of cake.

'I met a boy, actually,' she said, trying to sound casual. 'He said he knows you.'

'If he's from the village he's bound to. Everyone knows everyone round here. What boy?'

Emma shrugged. 'Called Tim.'

Lynda smiled knowingly. 'Oh yes? You've been chatting up Master Timothy, have you?'

'I wasn't chatting him up.'

'Not much! He don't talk first, that one. Well it won't get you anywhere. Our Debbie – she used to fancy him. She once got as far as holding his hand at The Lion disco and he ran a mile.'

'Who is he, anyway?' Emma asked, pouring herself some milk from a jug on the table.

'Don't drink all that. It's all that's left and the lads'll want their tea in the morning before the delivery.'

'I've only taken a bit,' Emma said, sipping the cold milk and munching at the cake.

Thunder rumbled in the distance outside the window and the sky was so overcast that the kitchen was almost in darkness.

'Who is he – this Tim?'

'Ah!' Lynda Carver grinned, knowingly. 'I could tell you were interested. Little madam! Sitting there as if butter wouldn't melt.'

Emma stared through the gloom at Lynda then, very deliberately, she grinned and winked.

'He is quite tasty, I have to admit!' she said in an unfamiliar, dreamy voice.

'Naughty, naughty! You're only a kid,' Lynda said, sounding mildly shocked. Then she lit a cigarette and drew deeply on it. 'Timothy Ransom – Doctor Ransom's lad. Funny, shy kid.'

'He didn't seem shy to me,' Emma bragged knowingly.

'Oh, didn't he indeed! Our Debbie will be furious. How old are you, anyway?'

'Old enough,' Emma said and smiled again. She hated how she was behaving. It wasn't her. She didn't recognize herself. But she knew exactly what was going on. It was her head-voice taking control. It had never happened quite like this before although she'd sometimes thought it was going to. Now that it was happening she sensed a new power;

a feeling of superiority, of being in charge of the situation. She was quite coolly manipulating Lynda – making her like her. What's more it was working. Lynda was visibly relaxing and warming towards her. And although Emma might claim that she didn't like what was happening, she didn't want it to stop either. It was like a fascinating game or like being an actress fully in command of the part she was playing and yet able to watch herself going through the motions at the same time.

'Go on – tell us about Timothy,' she said, wheedling like an expert. Then she gave a little, friendly laugh. 'Chronic name, isn't it? Timothy!'

Lynda shifted her weight in her chair and settled more comfortably.

'His father is Doctor Ransom,' she said, using the hushed tones of an intimate. 'They moved here – from York, I think it was – when Tim was just a baby. . . . Mind, Tim's not had it easy.'

'Why?'

'Because of his mother,' Lynda replied, sounding surprised that Emma didn't know.

'What about his mother?'

'Well, she's not well, is she?' Lynda lowered her voice, as if afraid to say the word. 'Cancer. They say she's got it everywhere. She's been fighting it for a year or two now. In and out of hospital. All the new fangled treatments. Sometimes she looks a bit better – but she's gone down badly this last year, apparently. Terrible to see her. . . .'

So that was why he was going to change her library books, Emma thought and immediately felt ashamed for having mocked him. But it wasn't her that had mocked him, of course. It was the other Emma – and almost at once that Emma pushed back into her head and she didn't feel ashamed any more. She just guzzled her milk and swung her legs and waited for Lynda to continue.

'Where'd you see him, any road?' Lynda asked, flicking ash from her cigarette into the saucer of her cup.

'He was by the pond.'

'Oh, was he indeed!' Lynda said with a satisfied nod. 'Well, he has no right to be "by the pond". It's all private land round the house, as he very well knows.'

'He was fishing.'

'Fishing! Stealing more like. Helping himself to private fish from a private pond. . . .'

'He says this house is haunted,' Emma cut in, making her voice sound matter-of-fact and unimpressed.

Lynda stopped in mid-sentence. They stared at each other.

'Is it?' Emma asked at last.

'How should I know? I don't live here, do I?' Lynda snapped and she stubbed out her cigarette and gathered up the dirty mugs and took them over to the sink.

'You spend a lot of time here,' Emma insisted. 'You'd be quite likely to know. Tim says it was your dad who told him.'

'Tim says . . . Tim says. . . .'

Emma shrugged. 'I just thought it was interesting, that's all.'

Lynda turned to face Emma. She seemed to make a conscious effort to sound calm. 'Look, lass. This is a big house and often I'm here on my own. Yes, I think it has a funny feel to it. But nothing more than that. So don't you go worrying about it . . .'

'Have you actually seen anything?'

'What d'you mean, seen?'

'A ghost,' Emma exclaimed, irritated by Lynda's deliberate evasiveness.

'No! Of course I haven't,' the older woman snapped but sounding far from certain. Then, looking flustered, she crossed and switched on the light.

'You have, haven't you?'

'Not me, no,' Lynda replied, returning to the sink.

'But your father did,' Emma said, rising and crossing to stand beside her.

'Oh, it's ancient history,' Lynda said running water into the sink. 'Fetch us your cup and plate. Go on, you can help me with this washing-up. . . .'

'Lynda! Please,' Emma pleaded.

'What?'

'Just tell me about the ghost,' she said, putting her plate and mug with the other dirty crocks and then picking up a tea towel to dry the dishes.

'You can ask any of the locals – they all know about it. . . .'

'I'm asking you,' Emma insisted and when Lynda glanced at her she flashed a smile.

The older woman began to wash the crockery with nervous, hurried movements.

'I hate the story myself. I always have. It makes me feel all jumpy about working here.'

'But it's just a story, Lynda . . .' Emma said. 'I mean we don't have to believe it if we don't want to.'

'Mmmh! It's easy to say that. But it gets a hold of you. The other day – when you came out of the bathroom – I thought I was going to have a heart

84

attack! The shock, you see? I didn't know anyone was up there. . . .'

'Go on. Tell me about it,' Emma surprised herself by putting a hand on Lynda's arm and giving it a friendly squeeze. 'I love being scared.'

Lynda Carver looked at her again and then she smiled.

'You kids! You're all the same. All right then. Mind, this all took place years ago – long before I was born. When Dad was no more than a kid himself. . . . He used to work here, you see. When the Westlakes still owned the place.'

'Who were they?'

'Local landowners. The Westlake family lived in this house for generations.'

'Why did they sell up?'

'They didn't. Not exactly. More "died off", if you see what I mean. Old Mr Westlake, the last one, he never married – so he was the end of the line. It was him my dad worked for. Then – after he died – the house just stood empty for ages – right until the Shawcross family moved in – and that's not more than ten years since.

'Anyway, Dad was a gardener here – one of four and, like I say, he was just a lad. It was all outdoor work he did. Never set foot inside the house except for one day in the year only and that was Christmas Eve when all the staff used to be brought into the front hall. There'd be a Christmas tree reaching all the way to the roof, covered with little candles – and they didn't have sprinklers and fire alarms in those days, you know. It must have been awfully dangerous – but pretty, a sight to see. Anyway, where was I? Oh yes – they'd all file in and stand in a line, with their caps in their hands, nervous

85

and shy. They'd each be given a mug of tea and a bit of cake. Mr Westlake did all the pouring and the serving. The idea was that for that one moment of the year – the servants were treated as the gentry. Then old Mr Westlake, he'd make a speech thanking them for all their hard work over the year – always the same speech every year.'

'Did he live here all alone?'

'Our dad?'

'No, Mr Westlake.'

'Oh, old man Westlake. More or less. He had a housekeeper called Ettie Styles. The gossip was they were lovers, but,' Lynda shook her head, 'my dad reckons that that was just talk. As he got older most of the house was shut up. He only used this kitchen and the room above as a bedroom. He'd sit all day with his chair pulled up to that range and the oven door open for extra warmth – summer and winter, always the same. They get very cold, the old. It's the same with Dad now. Always complaining about the draughts, no matter how warm the house is. . . .'

'The ghost, Lynda,' Emma cut in, stopping the flow of chatter.

'Why are you so interested, anyway?'

'Well, of course I am. Anyone would be. It's not every day you get to stay in a haunted house.'

'Have you seen something, then?' Lynda asked, turning and looking at Emma closely.

Emma shook her head and walked away, drying a plate absent-mindedly.

'No. Not exactly, no.'

'What then?'

'Just like you . . . a funny feeling.'

'Oh, for Dad it was more than any feeling. He says he saw.'

86

'What?'

'A figure – at one of the windows, when the house was empty. In the room where the builders are. He saw a little boy. Well, it all fits, you see. Old-fashioned clothes, mop of curly hair. It all fits.'

'Fits what?' Emma asked, her hands beginning to shake and her body to tremble.

'Dad was down on the front court, brushing up leaves. Mind, this was years and years ago – Dad was no more than a teenager. He looked up and saw this little boy. He was standing up on the window ledge, banging his fists against the window. His mouth was moving, as if he were shouting out, screaming almost . . . hysterical, you know. Well Dad were shaken of course. I mean it wasn't just a glimpse. He went on and on seeing – it was like as if the boy was screaming for help. Eventually Dad ran round to this door and came rushing in. He told Ettie Styles what he'd seen. She told him to go and get on with his work – fair lost her temper with him, she did. Then, soon after, Mr Westlake gave him his notice. He said he were cutting down on staff. So Dad went to work at the Pease estate over at Little Dale. Mr Westlake gave him a good reference and to tell the truth I think Dad were glad to get away.'

For a moment there was silence in the room. Then Lynda looked at her watch and hurried to dry her hands on the towel hanging over the Aga.

'And speaking of getting away, just look at the time. I'd best be off. It's your fault, keeping me talking. . . .'

'What did you mean, "it all fits"?' Emma asked.

'Well, with the murder and everything. It was the little Westlake boy he saw, Dad's always been

87

sure of that. Young Stephen Westlake, old Mr Westlake's brother – him that was murdered.'

3

The storm finally broke soon after Lynda had gone
home. Emma was still in the kitchen, staring at the
newspaper that had been left on the table without
really reading it, when a crash of thunder which
seemed to come from somewhere directly overhead
shattered the stillness. It was so loud that it shook
the mugs on the dresser. At the same time a sudden
wind sprang up, slamming the back door with a
resounding bang.

The kitchen light dipped ominously, flickered a
few times, and then went out. Near darkness envel-
oped the room. Emma crossed to the sink and
looked out of the window. Rain was lashing down
outside, jumping off the flagstones and overflowing
the gutters of the outhouses on the other side of
the yard. The acid yellow of lightning cut the sky
momentarily with its jagged lines, followed by more
thunder.

Emma went out into the back hall and tried the
light switch there – but without any success. All the
electricity in the house seemed to have been cut off.
Then, just as she was turning to go back into the
kitchen, she heard footsteps on the back staircase.

'Mum?' she called.

The steps faltered for a moment, then continued
– going away from her, up towards the top of the
house.

Emma hurried to the bottom of the stairs and
leaned against the banister rail looking up into the
gloom.

'Mum!' she called again. 'Is that you?'

The steps stopped at once. Emma waited, her heart racing, holding her breath and straining to hear any telltale sound. But now there was only a throbbing silence and the distant rumbling of the thunder.

She was on the point of returning to the kitchen when a slight movement higher up the stairs caught her attention. There was insufficient light for her to be sure, but vaguely through the gloom she thought she could see a figure leaning over the banister, staring down. Almost – but not quite; there – and yet not there. Was she seeing something? Or was it her imagination playing tricks? The more she stared, the less she was certain.

Taking a slow breath in an attempt to calm her racing heart, she started to climb upwards. After she had gone a few steps she stopped, listening intently. The only sound was the distant storm and the lashing rain outside the stairwell window. Looking up she could see . . . not a figure exactly but a gathering of substance . . . a darker shade in the gloom above her.

Her mouth was very dry and now she noticed her breathing. It seemed deafeningly loud, louder than the storm, filling the stairwell with its noise. She started to move again, keeping her eyes fixed on the shadow . . . the shade . . . the ghost . . . whatever it was that was leaning over the banister only a flight above her.

A long peal of thunder was followed by more flashing lightning. Its unexpected brilliance filled the stairwell. In this luminous glare Emma watched, spellbound, as the shadow resolved into the figure of a young boy, staring down at her. He was wearing an open necked shirt and his hair was a mass of dark, untidy curls. But it was his expression that made Emma gasp. The boy was staring at her with a look of such open, malicious glee – as if he were enjoying some horrible joke. A joke that was somehow directed at her.

The sudden sound of high, giggling laughter cut the silence, coming from somewhere just behind where Emma was standing, so close it seemed almost in her ear. She swung round, raising her hands instinctively, as if to ward off a blow, and nearly lost her footing on the stairs in her agitation.

But there was no one there, of course, and when Emma turned back the lightning had faded and the figure above her on the stairs had disappeared back into the gloom.

Emma shook her head, as if desperately trying to clear her mind of a thought or memory.

'Imagination,' she whispered to herself. 'Nothing but imagination.' She took another steadying breath and forced herself to continue climbing the stairs. She came to the narrow half-landing where double doors led to the first floor of the main part of the house. Then, turning the corner on the stairs, she was faced by the final steep flight to the top floor and the servants' quarters. Ahead of her was the place where she had imagined the figure. She made herself keep going forward and upwards. She noticed that she felt terribly cold. She shivered, the shock running right through her body. Taking another step . . . and then another . . . she climbed slowly to the precise spot where she had seen the boy standing.

There wouldn't be anyone there she told herself because it had all been in her imagination. . . . It

90

must have been. . . . But now she felt so horribly cold – as though an icy shaft of bitter wind was swirling round and through her. The sound of the thunder was far away and remote, the drenching rain a distant accompaniment.

Emma hesitated. She reached out to the banister rail, supporting herself.

Then she pulled her hand away with a terrified gasp. The place she had touched was warm. With a sickening lurch of consciousness she knew that she had placed her palm onto the back of a small, bony hand. Terror overwhelmed her. It drenched her in cold sweat. It snatched at her breath and made her legs tremble so that she thought she would collapse. With an immense surge of energy she pulled herself away from the spot – like a person escaping from quicksand or the sucking power of a raging torrent. Only her determination to be away from the unseen hand made it possible for her to get free. She staggered forward, slipping and tripping on the steps as she hurled herself upwards towards the top landing.

Once there she stopped again gasping for air and gripping the banister for support. She could hear light footsteps running away from her on the other side of the door that separated her from the top corridor.

A sudden and unexpected anger swept over her. She was determined to find out what was going on. She threw herself against the door and pulled it open.

'Who are you?' she screamed.

As she did so Harriet appeared as if from nowhere coming towards her and they collided, knocking each other against the walls of the corridor, in a flurry of arms and gasps and sudden, surprised expletives.

'Em!' Harriet said crossly, only just saving herself from falling over completely. 'Do look where you're going, darling!'

'You!' Emma gasped. 'What are you doing here?'

'I came to find you. The boys are packing up for the day. . . .'

'But – I thought you were with them.'

'I was. I came up the nursery stairs. I thought you'd be in your room.'

'Was it you on these stairs just now?' Emma shouted, her voice trembling. 'Why didn't you answer me?'

'I don't know what you're talking about,' her mother sounded bewildered. 'I've only just come up from the other wing.'

'Up these stairs?' Emma insisted.

'No! Up the nursery stairs. I've just told you that. Why don't you listen . . . ?'

'Mother! Those stairs go into my room,' Emma cried, turning her fear into anger and rounding on Harriet. 'I don't want you going in and out. It's my room.'

'It isn't your room!' Harriet snapped. 'It's just the one you happened to be given when we arrived. If you want to swop that's OK by me.'

'The door to those stairs is meant to be kept locked. Lynda Carver said so. They're steep and . . . dangerous.'

'I'm not a child, darling, so please don't talk to me as if I am! They make a useful short cut. I've got all my things up here. I need somewhere to use as a work place. . . .'

The overhead lights flickered and sprang into life.

'Oh, thank God!' Harriet said. 'The thought of spending the evening in the dark, locked in conversation with you in your present mood was not a happy one!'

'You don't have to talk to me,' Emma shouted, hurrying away from her along the corridor. 'You don't usually, so why start now?'

'Oh, Em! Please! I'm sorry. Truce, Emma! Please. . . .'

'Just leave me alone!' Emma yelled and she went into her own room and slammed the door.

As soon as she switched on the light she saw that the stair door was open. She went quickly to it and closed and locked it. Somehow the gaping opening added to her sense of fear and desperation. She withdrew the key and turned, breathing greedily as if she were suffocating. The room seemed unbearably warm and airless.

The landing door swung open slowly and Harriet appeared, leaning against the door frame, looking at her.

'Truce?' she said, raising a hand.

'There's something funny going on, Mummy,' Emma sobbed and she started to cry.

'Darling,' Harriet said, crossing and putting her arms round her daughter. 'What's the matter?'

'Nothing,' Emma shook her head, pushing away from Harriet and crossing to the dressing table. 'Nothing. I'm all right.' She took a tissue and blew her nose noisily.

'Doesn't look like nothing to me.'

'Oh, you know what I'm like!' Emma said with a shrug, trying to make light of the situation.

'You're bored, that's your trouble,' Harriet said, crossing and looking out of the window at the rain-drenched evening. The storm had abated. Dark clouds hung low over the distant hills. 'Why don't we go out tonight . . . I don't mean with Simon. Just the two of us.'

'I don't want to, honestly. The thought of a pub really bores me.'

'Let's go to a movie.'

'Where? We're in the middle of the country, Mother.'

'There must be a cinema somewhere! There's a local paper down in the kitchen. I'll go and look.'

Harriet went eagerly towards the door, glad to have something to do. Emma watched her in the dressing table mirror. She knew Harriet was trying to be kind and she was grateful for it. She didn't particularly want to go out, but neither did she want to stay in the house on her own. Really what she wanted was to be able to tell Harriet what was going on. But she knew that that would be impossible. Harriet wouldn't believe any of it. She scarcely believed it herself. So she sat silently watching as her mother moved as if in slow motion across the room. Then, reaching the door, she turned and said with a puzzled smile:

'Extraordinary smell that is. Have you noticed? Lavender and old roses. A sort of old ladies' scent. It's probably the polish Mrs Carver uses. It's terribly strong in here. . . . Come down, won't you? I'll make some supper and see if I can find a movie. . . .' She went out, leaving Emma sitting at the dressing table in a room smelling of the past.

DIARY

I will not go mad. There is a perfectly reasonable explanation for everything that's happening. It's all in my imagination. OF COURSE I saw a little boy! Lynda Carver had just told me in great detail all about how her father had seen him at the window when he was young and used to work here. So, as she was telling me, I was already starting to imagine him. He was waiting for me because I'd already made him up in my mind. Yes, that's it. I was having a sort of 'literal day dream' (like a dream you have in sleep transferred into being awake). I happen to have a powerful imagination, that's all! But knowing that doesn't really make it much better – because when I was imagining it it might just as well have been real. And what about the laughter? I really did hear that. I'm sure I did. I keep hearing it. Is that imagination too? Nor did any of it make sense. The laughter should have come from the boy ghost (or whatever I call it). Instead it came from behind me. It was so close it was right on my shoulder. Or am I just making that up as well? It was like as if the ghost sort of . . . jumped from one position to another. Now steady Emma. You're trying to make it real. You're trying to be logical about it. It doesn't work – trying to be logical about a dream. Because that's what this is. It's all a dream.

I'm so scared.

The hand was real. The hand was real. No, Emma! It couldn't have been. None of it was real.

Except the smell. . . .

When Mum mentioned that smell – that finished me completely – because I could smell it too. I still can. It's everywhere. A musky, old-fashioned 'granny smell'. Not like Muti though! Not a smart Rive Gauche *type of smell. This is an old-fashioned, ancient smell. And the thing is I know precisely where it comes from. I just know. It's her – the governess. And of course this room reeks of it – because it's her room. But she's been dead for a hundred years Emma. How can she still be filling the room with her scent? But MOTHER SMELT IT AS WELL. SO IT ISN'T MY IMAGINATION THIS TIME. Help. I've got to calm down. I've got to . . . make sense.*

WHAT I SO FAR ACTUALLY KNOW:
There was a murder here at Borthwick Hall. The victim was a little boy – the brother of the old man who was the last of the Westlake family to live here. I think Lynda C. said his name was Stephen Westlake . . . Why Stephen? That's Dad's name. Am I making all this up as well? NO. . . . This has all been told to me by Lynda. And Tim.

Tim also said there'd been a murder here (he says his mother knows the details).

Lynda's father thought he saw a ghost of a little boy at a window in the Games Room/Billiard Room – whatever it's called. And now I've seen the same ghost. (I IMAGINE I have.)

Just read all this back! I'm obviously out of my skull! What do I think I'm doing?? It's obvious it's my imagination working overtime. Pure fantasy! Probably something to do with 'hormones'! Part of the 'growing up process' that Mother blames for practically everything I do and feel.

LATER
My shoulder was hurting again. I just went and looked at it in the mirror. A scab is forming over it but it still looks pretty grotty. I can't really claim that it looks very artistic. It's more like a squashed spider than a star. I wish it'd stop throbbing. Incredible – that evening in the

bathroom at Talliser Road seems a hundred years ago. I wish I was there now – at home.

There's something really comforting about the middle of London – all those people and cars and muggings and bomb scares keep you in the real world. You don't need your imagination with all that going on. If I lived here permanently I think I'd be in a mental home by now.

THINGS TO DO:

Find out who did the murder. Lynda's dad might know – or Tim's mother

Try to get to see Lynda's dad

Try to get to see Tim's mother

See Tim? Maybe he could get me some antiseptic cream for my shoulder if it doesn't get better

See Simon Wentworth? Why on earth would I want to do that?

Put Mother off Simon. I can't have HIM as a stepfather. NO WAY!

Write to Father

Go to sleep

Can't sleep. The smell of lavender and roses is almost making me sick. I've had to open the window even though it's still raining.

Five

1

Emma woke suddenly. She lay with her eyes open staring at the dark. Something was different, something was missing. There was no sound of distant traffic. There was always traffic. However late it was it never stopped. Where, she used to wonder, did all the cars go to – particularly in the middle of the night? But now there was only silence, miles and miles of silence spreading out from her in every direction. A great blank world. An empty space.

Then she remembered where she was and a trickle of fear ran down her back, making her shiver and pull the sheet closer round her shoulders.

As her eyes gradually grew accustomed to the darkness, vague shapes began to form. She was lying on her side, facing away from the door. She could see the curtains blowing in the breeze from the open window. She remembered opening it earlier to get rid of the smell of the governess and then never closing it again.

The memory of the governess frightened her. She forced her mind to recall the evening instead.

They had driven to a cinema in an anonymous

town and sat side by side in a half-empty auditorium watching a film they'd both seen before.

'This is getting to be a habit,' Emma had observed, remembering the film she had watched on television the night they arrived.

'That's the trouble with the provinces!' Harriet had said, sounding like a character from an Oscar Wilde play. 'They never have anything new.' And they'd both giggled a lot and guzzled popcorn and behaved like children.

Afterwards they'd had a Chinese meal and then driven all the miles back over the sprawling moors through the obscuring night to the valley and the dark brooding house.

'Home!' Harriet had said as she turned the car into the back drive and it crunched up the gravel and through the tunnel to the yard.

'If only it was,' Emma had murmured.

They'd had a drink, sitting in the uncomfortable kitchen – squash for Emma and a 'zonking whisky' for her mother. It was as if they were reluctant to go to bed, as if there were things that were waiting to be said.

Harriet had seemed particularly nervous and on edge. She drank her whisky in gulps and talked too fast. She told Emma how the work was going and went into elaborate details about colour schemes and curtain materials and all the time it was as if she wanted to say other things and was . . . what? . . . afraid. But afraid of whom? Of what? Of her daughter?

Emma meanwhile wanted to say: 'I saw a ghost on the stairs' and 'I think this place is haunted' and 'Did you know there was a murder here, Mother? A little boy . . .' and 'Please help me. I'm so . . .

99

scared!' But none of the words were spoken. Why? Was she as afraid of her mother, she wondered, as her mother seemed to be of her?

Eventually they'd gone upstairs and parted in the corridor with a bright 'good night' and a joke about living in the servants' quarters and had then bumped into each other again in the bathroom, where they went to clean their teeth, and even then they both wanted to say something, to reach out to each other, to ask each other for help, but were unable to do so.

Emma had returned to her room agitated and depressed. She felt completely on her own. There was no one anywhere she could speak to. No one in the whole, rain-drenched, black world. The atmosphere in the room was stifling, the cloying scent of lavender and roses overpowering. She'd gone to the window and taken great gulps of the damp night air. She'd felt hot and cold at the same time, drowsy and awake, frightened and bored. Eventually she'd crossed to the double bed and climbed into the side of it nearest to the window.

Now, in the dark, Emma closed her eyes and tried to go back to sleep.

The sound started at once. One moment it hadn't been there, the next it was. A strange, bubbling, rasping sound; low and rhythmical; coming from somewhere horribly close to her.

She turned onto her back, listening intently. The sound was coming from somewhere so near to her that she knew with a terrible certainty that it – whatever was making the noise – was on the bed with her.

A slow, dribbling, damp noise. An indulgent, heavy breathing.

Then, unexpectedly, she felt a weight pressing down on her chest. She held her own breath, sudden fear paralysing her.

There was something heavy and living lying on top of her. After a moment it started to move, to crawl stealthily up the bed along the line of her body. The dribbling, bubbling, moist, still unrecognizable noise was growing louder and louder. She was fighting for air. Panic seemed to have attacked her brain. She couldn't even remember how to breathe. Then a wet, cold, unfamiliar . . . thing pushed itself against her face.

Emma choked, suffocating, a strangulated sound. She wanted to scream, to cry out for help. It was as if she were tied and bound by the terrible living creature that was covering her, rubbing its furry body against her mouth and nose, stopping her breathing as it smothered her with its warm, purring body.

'A C A T!' she screamed. 'A C A T! Mummy, Mummy! Help me! Help me! There's a cat!'

The purring grew steadily louder until it filled the room with its stifling presence.

Emma could feel the last of her breath being squeezed out of her. She was swooning for air, her lungs, savage and painful, seemed on the point of bursting. But still the body of the cat weighed down on her face, soft and heaving, preventing her escape.

'Help me! Help me!' she sobbed as she started to sink beneath the warm fur blanket into a spiralling fall through grey shadows that sucked at her, swirling and covering.

Then, way up above, somewhere out of sight at the top of the dark pit, she heard a voice calling:

'Emma! Emma! It's all right, darling!' it said,

shouting to be heard through all the suffocating layers that covered her. 'It's a dream, darling. It's only a dream. Wake up!' the voice begged and, as she fought her way up from the bottom of the pit she could see Harriet reaching down towards her with outstretched arms.

The arms encircled her, pulling her off the pillow and hugging her close. She gasped in great gulps of night air from the breeze blowing through the window.

'You were having a nightmare,' Harriet said and she put her hand on Emma's brow. 'Darling! You're baking hot. Are you running a temperature?'

'I don't know,' Emma said, shaking her head. 'There was a cat. . . .'

'No, darling. It was just a dream!'

Emma gasped again, her own breath bubbling and wheezing like the cat's had been.

'Oh, no!' Harriet exclaimed. 'Your chest sounds dreadful. Oh, darling!'

'What's the matter with me?' Emma whispered.

'I think maybe you've got asthma,' Harriet said. 'Oh, damn! You're not starting that again, are you?'

'There was a cat,' Emma insisted.

'No, darling. Honestly, you were dreaming. Sssh, baby! It's all right. It's over now.' And Harriet gently mopped her brow.

'Why would I dream about a cat?' Emma demanded. 'I don't even like cats.'

'Like them? Of course you don't! It's hardly surprising – when you were a baby you were nearly killed by one.'

'I was?'

'Well, maybe that's a bit of an exaggeration. But

102

you were terribly allergic to them. Don't you remember?'

Emma shook her head, then looked round the room, searching for the cat, certain that – no matter what Harriet said – somewhere it was hiding, watching her, waiting to pounce.

'We had a cat when you were little. You won't remember. It was when you were very young.'

'What happened to it?'

'I had to get rid of it.' Harriet frowned and shook her head as if she were remembering something unpleasant. 'You had terrible asthma when you were little,' she explained. 'Can't you remember any of this? It seems no time ago. I took you to see a specialist. He decided that it could be the cat that was causing it.'

'Asthma?'

'You had it very badly. Then you grew out of it. Actually, I think the specialist – his name was Gilchrist – I think he was right. When Beerbohm went, you started to improve almost at once.'

'Beerbohm??'

'The cat!' Harriet smiled.

'We had a cat called Beerbohm? Typical!'

'Actually it was your father's cat. When I married him,' she shrugged, 'I married the cat as well.'

'And when Dad left . . . ?'

'The cat stayed.'

'Honestly! Imagine leaving your pet behind. Didn't he love anything, my father – apart from himself, of course.'

'Well, he had to leave Beerbohm, really,' Harriet said in a measured, reasonable tone. 'He had no choice. He was going to America.'

'Is that why you got rid of it, Mother? Because it belonged to Dad? Poor cat!'

'No,' Harriet replied, a hard edge coming into her voice. 'I got rid of it because it was giving you asthma.'

There was silence for a moment.

'All right then – did it give me asthma because it belonged to Dad?'

'I don't know. It was your asthma, not mine. You tell me.' Her mother's face had taken on the strange, sullen, closed expression that always happened when her ex-husband was mentioned. Emma stared at her thoughtfully for a moment.

'Why will you never talk about him?' she asked.

'Because there's nothing to say,' Harriet replied, looking away from her.

'You have to forgive him sometime, Mother. Whatever he did.'

'Why?' Harriet asked, and she looked back, staring at her daughter coldly.

'Can't be good for you all that hate,' Emma mumbled. The cold eyes made her nervous.

'Well, maybe that's all coming to an end,' Harriet said, standing up quickly and moving nervously away from the bed.

Emma frowned.

'What d'you mean?' she asked.

'Not now,' Harriet said. 'We'll talk about it tomorrow.' She moved towards the door. 'Would a couple of aspirin help?'

'No, I'm all right now,' Emma said, still watching her mother closely.

'Let me put these behind you,' Harriet, said, taking the pillows from the other side of the double

104

bed and putting them behind Emma. 'It helps the breathing if you're sitting up a bit.'

'What's going on, Mother?' Emma asked, as Harriet fussed with the pillows behind her back.

'Nothing!' Her voice was firm. 'If you're really all right, I'm going back to bed. I've got a busy day tomorrow.'

Emma watched her as she walked back to the door. She wanted to stop her. She wanted to make her talk. She wanted, for some peculiar, unaccountable reason, to hurt her; to make her react; to force her to attend to her instead of running away.

'What did you do with Beerbohm?' she asked.

It seemed an innocent question but Harriet turned and looked at her with such a sad expression.

'He died,' she said.

'How?' Emma asked. She felt strangely apprehensive as she waited for the answer.

'I had him put down,' her mother replied.

'You killed him? Couldn't you have found another home for him?'

'No. It wasn't possible,' Harriet said.

'Did you try?'

Harriet hesitated for a moment, then she shook her head. 'I'm not going to talk about it now. I'm going to bed,' she said. 'Call, if you need me,' and she went quickly out of the room leaving the door ajar.

2

She must have slept because suddenly it was daylight and she hadn't been aware of any time passing. She lay propped up on the pillows, her head throbbing and hot. Her breathing was still very wheezy and constricted. Her body was aching.

'It's probably just a summer cold – or flu maybe,' Harriet said bringing her a jug of water and a bottle of squash. 'You're sure you don't want anything to eat?'

'No. I'm not hungry,' Emma told her. 'I expect I'll sleep a bit.'

'Your breathing sounds better than it was.'

'Does it? I feel pretty awful, actually!'

Harriet felt her brow. 'Don't be too impressed,' she said with a shrug, 'I don't really know what the hell I'm doing. This is just a token gesture!' Then as she continued to speak she mixed a glass of squash. 'When people are ill I feel their foreheads and when the car won't start I look under the bonnet. But the therapy in both cases ends there. I haven't a clue what I'm feeling for or what I'm looking at! So – if you're not any better by lunchtime I'd better ask Mrs Carver where we can find a doctor.'

'He's called Ransom.'

'Who is?'

'The local doctor.'

'How on earth d'you know that?'

Emma shrugged.

'Like your friend,' she said, 'I've been doing research!'

'Friend?' The nervous expression had returned to Harriet's eyes.

'You know, Mother, the dreaded Simon!' Emma said, with an innocent smile. 'What's his other name again? Witless?'

'Wentworth,' Harriet corrected her, her voice crisp and dangerously calm.

'Wentworth!' Emma sang the name. 'How much is a Went worth? You planning to marry him, Mother?'

'Marry him?' Harriet looked nonplussed by her suggestion and then defiant. 'Is that so shocking for you?'

'You hardly know him. Unless, of course . . .' sudden realization dawning. 'Have you been seeing him? All during this last year?'

'Really darling!' Harriet said lightly, avoiding the question. 'You sound like my mother!'

'You have, haven't you?' Emma continued, with growing certainty. 'And now you think you want to marry him.'

'Is it beyond the realms of your imagination that I might one day want to marry again? Is it such a surprise?'

'Yeah, Mother! I'm fainting with the shock! I expect it'll devastate Muti as well!' She stared at Harriet for a moment and her mother held the look, an evasive, hostile light in her eyes. 'Surprise us?' Emma continued. 'You must really think we're dumb. You've only got to meet an impossible man and you're all set to marry him! We expect it now, Muti and I. We've been through it so often before. Honestly! You're lucky you've got us to save you from yourself.'

'Why d'you say he's impossible! You don't even know him.'

'We went to the ballet, didn't we?'

'One night sitting in a theatre hardly enables you to make a valued judgement about a person.'

They stared at each other coldly. Then Harriet turned away from the bed.

'I'm going to be up and down these stairs a lot

today,' she said, changing the subject and crossing to the door of the nursery stairs. 'I'll try not to disturb you.' The door was locked. Harriet turned back to Emma again, her expression still cold and challenging. 'This door's locked. Can I have the key?'

'On the dressing table,' Emma said.

'Emma!' she said, crossing the room. 'We're the only people here. You don't need to keep it locked.'

'Only people? The place is swarming with builders,' Emma said. wheezing loudly. 'They're working at the bottom of those stairs. I don't want them coming in here while I'm in bed, do I?'

But Harriet wasn't listening. She had already unlocked the door and was disappearing down the stairs. Moments later Emma heard the lower door being opened. The noise of hammering grew louder and a chatter of voices rose in welcome as her mother went into the room on the floor below. Then the door was closed and the sound was muffled once more.

Later Lynda Carver suddenly appeared from the corridor and Emma realized that she'd been sleeping again. Looking at her watch she found that the morning was half over and she hadn't noticed its passing.

'I just thought I'd come and see how you're doing,' Lynda said, coming in.

'I feel a bit better, thanks,' Emma replied, sitting up quickly, flustered by this unexpected arrival. As she did so, the nightshirt she was wearing slipped sideways.

'Whatever's that on your shoulder?' Lynda asked, darting forward. 'You've had a nasty bite by the look of it.'

108

'It's nothing. It's all right,' Emma told her, hastily covering her tattoo with the nightshirt.

'What was it?' Lynda asked, looking at her suspiciously.

'I don't know. A bite, I suppose. It's nothing. It doesn't hurt.'

'You want to put some antiseptic cream on it. Ooh, I say!' she exclaimed, cheerfully. 'Listen to your wheezing chest! It's bronchitis, that is. How did you get that?'

'It's just a cold. The thunder makes everything so airless,' Emma said, looking towards the window, 'that's why I'm finding it hard to breathe.'

'Not today. It's lovely and fresh. You should get yourself up. Go out for a bit. That's your trouble. Stuck inside all the time.'

'I was out all day yesterday,' Emma protested.

'I meant last night. The room was so stuffy and it had a funny smell.'

'These top rooms always get airless in summer,' Lynda said, ignoring her comment about the smell. 'Being under the eaves, I suppose.' As she spoke she crossed to the window, taking a packet of cigarettes and matches out of the pocket of her apron and lighting up, sucking contentedly at the smoke.

'Oh, I meant to ask you – is there a cat in the house, Lynda?' Emma said, slipping out of bed while the older woman's back was towards her and putting on a dressing gown. She felt at a disadvantage, lying in bed with Lynda in the room.

'Cat?' Lynda asked, looking round. 'No. They've got three dogs, the Shawcrosses. And both the girls have horses. But they don't have a cat. The animals all go over to Lady Shawcross' sister to be looked after while the family are away. Tell the truth they spend more time over there than they do here – what with all the toing and froing. But there are no cats. Never have been, not since the Shawcrosses moved in. Mind, when old Mr Westlake was alive the place was overrun with them. When he died the RSPCA had to come in to deal with them. Cats everywhere. I don't like them myself. I'm not keen on any animals in the house – but I'd rather have a dog than a cat.'

'I'm sure I heard one.'

'When?'

'In the night.'

'There are no cats in this house.' She pinched her cigarette out, holding her hand out of the open window, and threw the end onto the sloping roof. Then she turned, wiping her finger and thumb on her apron. 'You're getting up, are you?' she said, watching Emma as she went to the dressing table.

'I thought I'd have a wash.'

'Let's have a look at that bite.'

Taken off guard Emma wasn't prepared for the sudden movement. Lynda reached out and pulled aside her dressing gown and nightshirt. As she peered at the tattoo her face was so close that Emma could smell the smoke on her breath.

'Mmmh! Doesn't look like a bite to me. What have you been doing?'

'Nothing. I've been scratching it. Get off me!' Emma complained shrugging her away and covering herself again.

Lynda looked at her closely, then shook her head.

'You kids! We never know what you get up to,' she said. 'You want to stop worrying about ghosts and get yourself out. A nice walk, that'd do you far more good than stuck in this old house all day.

110

Right, I'm off. Your mother's up to her eyes in paint and all those lads are hammering away fit to bust. I'm going to make myself scarce. Nothing I can do with the house in such a mess.'

'Is that why you came up? To tell me you were leaving early?'

'I didn't want to disturb your mother. Say I'll see her in the morning.'

She walked back towards the door. Emma followed her, carrying her sponge bag.

'Lynda,' she said as they went out into the corridor. 'Can I come and meet your father sometime.'

'Dad?' Lynda Carver asked, looking surprised. 'Why would you want to do that?'

'I'd like him to tell me more about when he used to work here – about the ghost.'

'I shall wish I'd never told you if you don't stop going on about it,' Lynda complained.

'I'm bound to be interested. I've never stayed in a haunted house before.'

'It's not haunted. That was just another of Dad's stories.'

'Well I'd like to hear it for myself. Can I? Would you mind?'

'You can come and see him any time you want – but it won't do you any good. Dad's storytelling days are long over. He's gone senile. Been like it for years. No memory at all. He thinks I'm Mother half the time. When I say, "Dad, I'm your daughter!" he just shakes his head and smiles. Mind, we're very lucky. He keeps cheerful. A lot of old people get very depressed. Dad – he just laughs all the time. You can come and see him. He's always glad of a bit of company. But don't expect any sense

111

out of him. He won't be able to tell you anything. His brain's gone.'

DIARY

The cat was real. I'm sure it was. I'd know if I was dreaming. And if it wasn't a dream and it wasn't real – then what other alternative is there? That I'm being haunted by a cat as well as all the others?! But then LC said the house used to be overrun with cats when old Mr Westlake lived here. I nearly wrote Wentworth then. The names are similar . . . everything seems to be linking up. Maybe I'm really going mad. Like Lynda's father. He would be senile, wouldn't he? Just when he could have told me things. I wonder – did seeing the ghost all those years ago affect his mind? Did he think about it over and over again, like I'm doing now, all through his life until, in the end, it drove him mad? In which case I'd better be careful myself. Because I definitely saw the boy on the stairs. Which means I've already seen one ghost. Then there was the boy's hand that I touched. IF it was his – now, as I remember it, it felt too small to be the boy's hand – it was almost more like a baby's hand. What baby? Where did a baby come from all of a sudden? Another ghost??

How many ghosts am I claiming here?

GHOST LIST
1 The governess (Although when I saw her I was definitely dreaming – so maybe she doesn't count? BUT dream or not what I saw then told me more about what actually was going on than any of the other things . . . I mean, the room being a Billiard Room; the glasses used to dazzle and being responsible for the light I saw at the window.

112

*[TWICE – I've seen that light twice.] All that
information came from the one 'dream'.)
2 The boy on the stairs
3 The baby hand (not seen – but felt)
4 The cat on the bed
5 The running footsteps
6 The giggling
7 The whispering
8 The governess's scent
Only 1 and 2 were actual 'sightings' – all the others were
sounds and smells and feelings . . .*

*Just read through all the above. I hope no one else reads
it! It is the journal of a mad person!*

*Funny about the cat and me getting an asthma attack –
then Mother telling me about being allergic when I was
little and Dad's cat that she had put down . . . because of
me.*

Emma stopped writing. Her biro trembled between
her finger and thumb. She stared thoughtfully out
of the bedroom window at the evening light. Then
she started to write again:

*What if the cat is my ghost? I mean – what if it doesn't
belong to the house and the house's story so much as it
belongs to me and my story. It would make sense. Beerbohm
was put down because of ME. What better reason than
that is there for him/it to haunt me? And the laughter. I
do hear it. But I've heard it in my head for years – and
the whispering, come to think of it. There's often been a
voice talking to me. That other voice – the one I hear in
my head. I've never seen it as a ghost though. I mean, it's
just thoughts in my head going round and round and
mocking me. . . . Like as if I'm two people. A nice Emma*

113

and a nasty Emma. And sometimes – quite often – the two talk to each other. Well, not talk, but niggle and . . . mock. But now, since I've been here, it's like as though these two mes are becoming more separate. As if the inside one has broken free and has got outside my head. So I don't just imagine the laughter and the whispering . . . I'm beginning to really hear it.

Now I feel as if I'm beginning to haunt myself!

Six

1

That evening Emma felt well enough to go down-stairs for supper.

Harriet had prepared a salad and, because they had both been inside all day and the weather had turned bright and dry again, they decided to take their plates and a bottle of wine out into the garden. They ate sitting at a table on the terrace overlooking the lawns and flower beds, with the elaborate iron railings and the meadow beyond. Distantly the trees round the pond blurred into the haze as the evening light thickened and the sun set, golden and apricot, in an almost white sky. Birds were singing the eve-ning chorus and moths gathered round the lighted windows of the house behind them as the dusk settled.

Perhaps because of the beauty and peacefulness of the setting they seemed more relaxed in each other's company and after they'd finished eating and Harriet had poured herself another glass of wine she started to talk to Emma about her ex-husband in a way that she'd never done before.

'I always thought I should keep him from you,' she said, looking at the wine in her glass, then

115

holding it up so that the last of the light shone through it. 'Perhaps that was a mistake. I don't know. When we were together he wasn't famous, you see. That all came after. But of course, for you, he's always been the big star. When you think about him you can only be like one of the public. . . .'

'But I'm not!' Emma interrupted her. 'He's my father.'

'Yes. But nevertheless the man you think about . . . is the "film star", he can't be anything else now. When I think about him – which I try fairly hard not to do! – I remember before all that. "Stephen Hartley, the oldest hopeful in the business!" That's how he used to speak about himself. "I have good looks, a talent and I can't even get arrested" he used to say to anyone who cared to listen. He could be boringly bitter! Bitter and ambitious. He only ever wanted to be in films, you see. And then – if not the lead – it had at least got to be a "featured role". Television held no interest, because it wasn't big and showy enough – and as for the stage, it bored him. He knew precisely where he was aiming. "The top!" That's what he'd say. "It's the top or nothing!" Poor guy. It practically ate him hollow. When friends got jobs he'd be delighted for them – unless of course the job happened to be in a movie. When that happened . . . he dropped the friend. People probably thought it was the other way round – that the friend was too busy – but it was always Stephen's doing. I remember Michael James getting his first role – in a Nicholas Roeg film. Stephen was consumed with envy! He never spoke to Mike again and he took great delight in rubbishing his performance! He wanted only one thing out of life . . . to be what he is now,

116

I suppose – a star. If ever there was an example of "if you want something badly enough, you'll probably get it", it's Stephen's career. I wonder if it's given him any happiness?'

'Why not? He's doing what he wants to do and he happens to be very good at it.'

'True.'

'He gets great films playing the best parts – of course he's happy. He's got what he dreamed of.'

'But does that make you happy or is it the most dangerous thing that can happen to you? Look at Midas – all he wanted was that everything he touched should turn to gold. He got his wish literally . . . and starved to death.'

'I don't see the connection.'

'Well – when I first knew your father . . . yes, he wanted to be the "film star" but there was much more to him than that. He also wanted to travel. . . .'

'He does – making films!' Emma cried, like a card player, putting down an ace.

'And he wanted a family.'

'He's got several!'

They sat in silence for a moment, Harriet sipping her drink and staring out over the garden.

'It's only natural I should want to know him, Mother,' Emma said eventually. 'He's not only my father, he's also a very glamorous, famous person.'

'But what I'm saying is that I don't know that person any more than you do. He's certainly not the man I was married to – nor is he the man who fathered you.'

'I don't care. I still want to get to know him.'

'Then write to him again,' Harriet said, turning and looking squarely at Emma.

'I keep meaning to . . . but I put it off.'

'Because you're afraid of being rejected?'

Emma pulled a face. 'He was horrible the last time I tried,' she said.

'Well, I did warn you.'

Suddenly and unexpectedly Emma felt a lump forming in the back of her throat. She swallowed hard, blinking back the tears that had welled up into her eyes.

'I didn't know how to write the letter,' she said, looking away hurriedly in case Harriet saw she was on the point of crying. 'I put it all wrong.'

'There is no right or wrong way, darling,' Harriet said, her voice sounding kinder. 'Not for a letter like that.'

Again there was a long silence between them.

'He's a pig,' Harriet said, more to herself. 'Still a pig.'

'No. He just . . . wasn't expecting to hear from me. . . .'

'So he dictated his reply to a secretary and sent you a money order for a hundred pounds? The man is a louse!'

'Would you help me?'

'To do what? To write to him? I think I'd be worse at it than you. I do remember him, you see.'

'What he did to you – was it really so awful?'

Another long silence between them was underlined by the noisy squawking of the rooks in the pond trees.

'It was all a long time ago,' Harriet said at last.

'That's what you always say,' Emma protested.

'It's the truth. Look – when he finally left I told him I'd never willingly speak to him again and that

118

I wanted nothing from him. . . .' She shrugged. 'I still feel the same.'

'So – forgive him, Mother. Like you say, it was ages ago. . . .'

'Actually, darling,' Harriet said, her voice hard, 'you don't know what you're talking about.'

'Well, that isn't my fault. I keep asking you. . . . But we always end up having a row instead. That isn't fair, you know.'

'Life isn't!' Harriet said, a hint of anger creeping into her voice.

'I want a father!' Emma insisted, her voice beginning to tremble. 'I have the right to one. I'm here, you know. I do exist.'

'Believe me, it's entirely thanks to me that you do.'

'It takes two to make a baby, Mother!' Emma said, glibly.

She saw her mother flinch and then Harriet's back went tense as the temper that she had been keeping at bay exploded through her.

'If your father had had his way you wouldn't have been born,' she snapped.

'What d'you mean?' Emma asked, suddenly afraid.

'What d'you think I mean?' Harriet asked, sudden weariness in her voice. 'He wanted us to get rid of you.'

'No!' Emma said, raising her arms as though in self-defence.

'So much for your ever-loving father.'

'That isn't true,' Emma gasped. 'You're lying to me.'

Harriet sighed and looked away.

'That's why we parted,' she said, speaking more

119

calmly and with sudden regret. 'He told me my timing was bad. That babies would hold up his career. He'd just got his big break – the part in *Screwdriver*. He said babies . . . would get in the way.'

Somewhere very close Emma heard laughter. She looked round quickly, searching the dark shrubberies and the pale, hazy lawns.

'I can see how inconvenient I must have been. What did he suggest should be done?' she asked, keeping her head turned away from her mother.

'Let's leave it now, Em. Please,' Harriet said, reaching out and putting her hand lightly on her daughter's arm, her face filled with regret.

'What did he say you should do?' Emma insisted, pulling away.

Harriet shook her head and shrugged. Too much had been said to turn back. When she answered her voice was quiet and resigned. 'He wanted me to terminate the pregnancy.'

Emma got up quickly and ran down the steps of the terrace.

'Em!' her mother called, behind her. 'Don't run away. . . .'

'I'm not!' Emma said, brightly. 'I'm really not.'

'Where are you going?'

'I'm sure I heard someone laughing.'

'There's no one there. Come back, Em. Please! I'm sorry. I shouldn't have told you like that. I'm sorry. . . .'

'It doesn't matter,' Emma called. Tears were spilling down her cheeks but she managed to keep her voice steady. 'It really doesn't matter.' She had gone a long way down the lawn towards the iron fence. She wanted to be away from her mother, away from the truth.

'Emma,' Harriet called, singing the name like a distant echo.

Emma turned and looked back at her. She was standing away from the table, on the edge of the steps, staring out into the garden. 'Come back, please darling. Let me explain. Let me explain it all.'

'Nothing to explain,' Emma called. 'He didn't want a baby – that's all. Doesn't mean he wouldn't adore me now!'

Somewhere near to where she was standing a twig snapped. Emma turned quickly, searching the big bushes that lay beside her.

High giggling laughter broke the stillness of the night, so near that she could reach out and touch the person, if only she could see whoever it was.

'Emmy,' a voice whispered in the dark. 'Now we know, don't we, Emmy dear? Know what we've always known. Daddy didn't want us, did he? But that's nothing new. We've always known.'

'Go away!' Emma screamed. 'Go away and leave me alone!'

'Emma!' Harriet shouted, hurrying down the steps and running across the lawn towards her. 'Darling! Please!' And, as she spoke, her voice broke and she started to cry.

Emma turned and, as Harriet came towards her, she allowed herself to fall into her mother's arms. Harriet took all her weight, holding her in a strong embrace, supporting her and coaxing her back across the dark grass towards the lighted windows of the house.

'It's all right, baby. It's all right. I'm here. I'm

here,' she crooned gently and comfortingly. 'I shouldn't have told you like that – and it wasn't what you think. It was us. Stephen and me. It wasn't that he didn't want you. It was that he didn't want me any more. We'd grown apart. I was all right for him in the early days – then I could earn money and be useful to him. But when he saw success beckoning . . . I didn't fit in any more.'

As they climbed the steps up onto the terrace a face looked down from one of the first floor windows. Emma saw it quite clearly. It didn't even surprise her or frighten her. It seemed the most natural thing that it should be there. If she had been on her own she might even have waved to it and seen a hand raised in answer. She was looking at the pale features of a young boy with a mass of curly black hair. She recognized him at once. He was the boy she had seen on the stairs. He was looking out of a window at the far end of the house. It belonged to the room below hers. The nursery. The room the builders were working on. The room at the bottom of the stairs. He was standing there, looking out into the dark garden and he was staring straight at her. And although he didn't move, didn't gesture or wave, she somehow knew he was calling to her.

He's asking for my help, she thought. I think that's what he was doing on the stairs as well. He needs me.

Close behind her someone laughed, a high giggle. She spun round, breaking free from her mother's supporting arms.

'Did you hear . . . ?' she gasped.

'Yes,' Harriet said, with scarcely a glance over her shoulder. 'An owl, I think.' She started gathering the dishes on the table. She shivered. 'It's cold now. Let's go in.'

'I think I'll go back to bed, actually,' Emma said, staring along the length of the house to the window on the first floor where she could still vaguely see the shadow of the boy.

'Darling,' Harriet said, turning towards her. 'I've done something bad. I didn't mean to. . . .'

'No!' Emma said, kissing her unexpectedly on the cheek. 'It's good. Far better that we talk. . . .'

'I didn't mean he didn't want you. . . .'

'He didn't,' Emma said almost cheerfully. 'It's no big deal. It's not going to turn me into shrink material, I promise. I don't feel deprived, Mother. I just need to know these things. It's much better that you talk to me. Honestly. . . . But, d'you mind if we don't go on now? I feel whacked. I'll be asleep as soon as my head touches the pillow. . . .'

And so they carried the supper things back into the house and after a gentle parting Emma went up to her room. As she ran up the stairs she felt as if she was hurrying to see a friend.

2

Emma heard Harriet come into the room, leaving the door open so that light from the landing spilled in behind her. She watched her mother as she tip-toed towards the bed, then she closed her eyes and breathed deeply, feigning sleep. She felt Harriet run a hand gently through her hair and, moments later, she heard the door close again and when she opened her eyes that half-light had gone and the room was in darkness once more.

She heard Harriet go to the bathroom. Then the

landing lights were extinguished and she heard her mother go into her own bedroom and close the door.

Silence followed, but still she waited, lying in the warmth of her bed. Outside the open window the night air seemed to breathe and pale moonlight filtered into the room. As her eyes grew accustomed to the dark so more and more objects were discernible.

Night is never really dark, she thought, there's always some light and anyway once I get downstairs I can put on the electric lights if I get frightened. . . .

She pushed aside the memory of the lights going off in the hall and told herself that anyway, however afraid she might be, she had to go down to the nursery for the boy's sake.

He really wants me there, she thought. He needs me. That's why he was watching me. I'm sure of it. Then she frowned and shook her head. But why me? she wondered. What have I got to do with him, or this place, or . . . anything? It's pure fluke that I'm here at all. And yet it's as if he wants to tell me something . . . as if he's chosen me. Unless, of course, I'm the only one who is bothering to notice him. Maybe he's been trying to contact Mother and the builders and even Lynda Carter – after all, he once tried to contact her father. Emma yawned. All the activity in her head exhausted her. Maybe it would be best just to go to sleep and bother about it in daylight, she thought. There's a lot I need to find out. I'll go and see Tim's mother. He said she knows what went on here . . . about the murder and everything. . . .'

Thinking about the murder was a mistake. Immediately a shiver of fear wriggled down her back.

No! she thought. I must concentrate on the boy. . . . Then a sudden realization stopped her in mid-thought. He's scared, terrified. My ghost is more frightened than I am.

She sat up in bed, pushing away the protecting covers.

'I'm going down!' she said out loud, her voice sounding unfamiliar in the silent room.

As she got out of bed another thought occurred to her to which she gave no more than cursory attention. She simply noticed that the other voice, her head-voice, was missing. This was precisely the sort of situation that would have brought the voice, mocking and goading, and yet now it wasn't there. For most of her life she had suffered its whining commentary and cruel mimicry. Where had it gone? For a moment, as she climbed out of bed, she did think the disappearance was odd but then the moment passed and she didn't think about it again until much later.

She put on a dressing gown and slippers. She unlocked the door to the nursery stairs and pocketed the key. She felt more secure carrying it. She didn't want to be locked in on the stairs again.

The stairwell was very dark. She wished there was a light she could switch on. She was tempted to leave one on in her bedroom, as a beacon to welcome her back, but worried that her mother might notice the telltale glimmer under the door if she got up to go to the bathroom. As she didn't want Harriet to know what she was doing, she left her room in darkness.

Going down the steps was like going into a warm pit. She told herself that this was the worst part, that once she was down in the nursery there'd be

125

light from outside the window and more space. The stairs were particularly scary because she felt trapped by them, closed in on every side, suffocated. She had already been trapped there once. But if it happened again, now, there were no friendly builders around to come to her rescue. She could feel her courage wavering and her breathing started to wheeze as her chest tightened.

'Don't think about it. Just go down,' she told herself and she forced herself to run down the stairs without another pause.

The door at the bottom was closed. But it wasn't locked. Pushing it open she was greeted by a draught of fresh, cool air. She shivered as she stepped into the room.

The long windows allowed more light to enter in. She was amazed how easy it was to see things. The floor was littered with builder's equipment. There was a stack of the panelling boards that had already been removed from the walls in the centre of the room. More than half the walls had already been stripped. The dark, Victorian wood still remained round the windows and along the wall with the door in it, through which she had just emerged.

Emma was struck by how ordinary the room appeared. The courage she had needed to get down the stairs seemed hardly to be rewarded by the cluttered space and half-finished work that she found there.

She tiptoed to a window and looked out. She saw the pale, silvery garden and the stone terrace. Along at the far end was the table where she and Harriet had eaten supper.

The memory made her depressed. She didn't want to think about her father or about the conversation she had had at the table with her mother. In fact there were so many topics that were dangerous for her that it seemed most sensible not to think at all.

She turned her back on the window and leant against it, looking round slowly. She had a strange sense of anticlimax. It had taken all her strength and courage to come down the stairs and now she was here the place seemed so dull and uninteresting that she couldn't help being disappointed. What had grown in her mind into a haunted chamber full of ghosts and sounds and terrible unexpected happenings was just a room that was in the process of being altered by builders. It was a mundane, ordinary work place, smelling of dust and wood shavings with a hint of wet paint.

She walked slowly across to the main door, side-stepping a work box and a mound of loose plaster that had been swept into a pile, with the broom lying on top of it.

The smell of fresh paint was stronger as soon as she went out onto the main landing. The door opposite was wide open. She crossed and looked inside. The long Billiard Room was filled with pale moonlight. Here there were cans of paint and ladders and planks stacked against one wall.

She turned away and walked along the landing as far as the wide, square stairwell with the hall below. The night sky was tinged with a luminous glow outside the high window above the front doors. She could see trees moving restlessly against the sky, blown by an unheard breeze. Inside the hall, all around her, dark shadows were accentuated by the thin, filtered rays of an invisible moon. The silence was overwhelming.

127

Emma leaned against the banister rail and waited.

Nothing happened. There were no running footsteps, no high giggling laughter. Nothing.

'Hello!' she called. But no answer came back to her from the shadows. 'Is there anyone there?' she asked, her voice getting stronger. 'I'm not afraid. . . .'

She stayed on the landing until she was shivering with cold. The anticlimax was complete. Nothing happened. The whole expedition was a waste of time. Worse than that, she felt she had been made a fool of – or rather that she had made a fool of herself.

Eventually she went back to the nursery and crossed quickly to the dark stairs. As she started to climb them she could see the pale moonlight glimmering through the door at the top. She hurried up the steps two at a time and reached the small square landing breathless and wheezing, with her heart beating fast.

She went into the room and deliberately closed the door and locked it with the key from her dressing gown pocket. Then, taking the key, she put it on the dressing table. She walked towards the bed, slipping off her dressing gown and dropping it on the armchair as she passed it.

Finally she got into bed and turned on her side facing the window with the covers pulled up over her shoulders.

'A sheer waste of time,' she complained. 'Probably all I'll have achieved is another cold. I'll die of pneumonia or something and I'll come back as a ghost. The wheezing ghost of Borthwick!'

She was just dropping off to sleep when she felt

the first hint of a movement. It impinged upon her drifting mind, without immediately manifesting itself. . . .

She was dreaming, of course. Dreaming that there was someone in the bed with her. . . .

She could feel a warm, tense body pressing up against her. Whoever it was had got his or her back turned towards her. She was lying side by side and back to back with another occupant of the bed.

Then, with a sickening jolt, this vague, uncomfortable half dream became reality. The person started to push her. She could feel her body sliding across the bed.

'Mother?' she whispered, knowing it was foolish.

'Mother!' a voice echoed in her ear.

Emma turned quickly onto her back and then over onto her other side. She was looking straight at a familiar face, lying on the pillow next to her, staring at her. In the pale moonlight she saw the expression turn from questioning blankness into a hideous grin. Then with an unexpected dart two arms reached out towards her, pushing her away.

Emma grabbed the wrists, holding them in her clenched hands. They were stick-like and warm; thin, living wrists. She forced them back, her strength, charged by her own terror, amazing her. She forced the wrists back until the arms were flat on the pillow on either side of the terrible face. Now the other person's legs started to thrash and the body to squirm away from her. Emma held onto the wrists. Whatever happened she was determined that she would not let go. Gradually she pulled herself up on top of the wriggling, heaving body until she was sitting astride it. Then pressing her weight down onto the two wrists she forced them back onto the pillow again.

The face staring up at her was her own face.

She was fighting with herself.

The shock of recognition brought a scream up into her throat but before it could escape into the silent night she was distracted by the sound of laughter echoing round the room. She looked over her shoulder and saw a shadowy form moving between her and the open window.

The boy leapt at her waving his hands like a picture book ghoul, rolling his eyes and pulling a ghastly, leering face.

Emma shied away from him and as she did so she felt the body under her wriggle free. This sudden movement overbalanced her and she slid off the bed, landing heavily on her twisted legs. At once she pulled herself up using the bed covers as a lever until she was crouching beside the bed, peering over it. She watched the boy taking the key from the dressing table. Then he turned and ran towards the door to the nursery stairs. But Emma was nearer to it. She threw herself across the space getting there first. She saw the boy stop, a sharp intake of breath turning into a snarl as he confronted her.

Now a new event utterly confused Emma. From the opposite side of the room the same boy suddenly appeared again, running towards her. He seemed to be crying. He was holding out his hands to her. It was definitely the same boy. He had the same dark curly hair; he wore an identical white night-shirt. But now there were two of them. Emma looked from one to the other in disbelief. . . . The one with the key was grinning at her, lunging back-wards and forwards, close enough for her to touch him and then pulling away before she managed to do so. Between his finger and thumb dangled the key. He was holding it out to her, tempting her to come and get it. Unable to bear the game any longer, Emma made a grab for him, leaving her place beside the stair door. As she did so she saw him throw the key over her head. She turned in time to see the other boy, or the same boy – were there two of them, she didn't know – catch the key and dart towards the stairs, laughing wildly.

Emma was near the bedside table. She reached out and switched on the lamp.

As the light filled the room, the door to the nursery stairs swung shut.

Finally, gasping and exhausted, Emma turned and leaned against the dressing table. Very slowly she raised her eyes. She was staring at her reflection in the mirror. The face she saw she recognized as her own. But was it her own? Or was it the person she'd been fighting with on the bed who was now staring so calmly and coldly at her.

'Oh, God! Help me!' she gasped. 'Somebody please. . . . Help me!'

And as she sank to her knees in front of the dressing table, she saw the expression on the face in the mirror turn into a hideous grin and she heard the high, giggling laughter.

'Poor Emmy!' a voice said somewhere very close to her. 'Having a hard time, are you? We haven't started yet!'

Then everything went black; silent and black. There was no pain, no fear; nothing.

DIARY

I feel better today. Breathing less wheezy. I shall go out.

Last night was a terrible nightmare night. Probably due to my cold and running a temperature. Awful dreams – the sort you don't like to remember. So I won't! And they were only dreams so I refuse to get into a state about them.

Mother and I had quite an interesting conversation over supper about Dad. If she is to be believed he wanted her to get rid of me! The cheek!

> *'I care for nobody, no not I*
> *Cos nobody cares for me.'*

Seven

1

The surgery was in one wing of a large Victorian house, standing on the edge of Borthwick village. It was a joint practice with two other doctors named on the brass plate beside the door.

'I don't suppose it matters which one you see,' Harriet said as they went in. But Emma, who had only agreed to the visit in order to see Tim's father, persuaded her that if Dr Ransom was on duty it would be sensible to go to him as he'd been recommended.

This plan was however quickly negated by the receptionist, a grey-haired woman with spectacles, whom they found sitting, typing, in a space behind a counter in the waiting room. 'I'm sorry,' she said, 'Dr Ransom's not on duty today. Dr Rogers can see you. Do you have your medical card . . . ?'

The waiting room was empty but after a few minutes a woman with a small baby came in and sat opposite Harriet and Emma. The baby was in a grizzly mood, whimpering and snuffling and far from happy. Its mother held it high against her shoulder with one hand while she flicked through a magazine spread out on her lap with the other.

'Oh, Lynette!' she complained occasionally, rocking the baby up and down, patting its back. Then she glanced across and smiled shyly. 'She's teething! They never tell you at the prenatal what it's really going to be like, do they? Lynette!' and she rubbed the baby's back as if hoping somehow to soothe away her misery.

Later a man came out of the door marked *DOCTORS*. He was carrying a walking stick. He went over to the receptionist, limping badly, and leaned against the top of the counter.

'I've got to come back,' he said.

'I thought you'd have to,' the receptionist told him. Then she glanced out into the room. 'Right Joyce, you can go in,' she said, and the woman with the baby got up and disappeared through the door.

'We were next,' Emma whispered.

'She probably had an appointment,' Harriet told her, picking up an ancient copy of *Country Life* and flicking through the pages.

'How are you feeling then, Mr Carver?' the receptionist asked.

'How do you think?' the old man grumbled.

'Carver?' Emma whispered to Harriet. 'D'you suppose he's Lynda's dad?'

'Maybe,' her mother replied, without showing much interest.

'Is it still your legs?' the receptionist asked, without looking up from the form she was filling in.

'It's every bit of the blessed body,' the old man replied. 'Our Georgie gets all the sympathy – but he's got nowt to put up with like I have.'

'Next Tuesday, same time then,' the receptionist said and the old man trudged to the door, leaning heavily on his stick.

'You'll get my prescription done up . . .' he said, without looking back.

'Yes, don't you worry. It'll be ready for collection as usual.'

After the man had gone Emma rose and went to the counter.

'Excuse me,' she said. 'Was that Lynda Carver's father, can you tell me?'

'I thought I knew you,' the receptionist said with a smile, addressing Harriet, who had looked up, surprised by Emma's sudden move. 'You're the one who's working up at the Hall, aren't you?'

'I'm up there at the moment, yes,' Harriet replied warily.

'Must be nice to get a decorator in. I hate wall-papering myself.'

'So do I,' Harriet told her, looking back at her magazine and cutting off any further conversation. Being referred to as a 'decorator' always irritated her.

'Was he Lynda's father?' Emma asked again.

'No. Lynda's father is George. That was Mr Jack Carver.'

'Oh,' Emma said, disappointed. Then, as she returned to her seat, she added, 'Are they related?'

A phone started to ring.

'Georgie and Jack Carver?' the receptionist exclaimed, turning to answer it. 'Of course they are. They're brothers. Well, more than that really – they're twins! They used to be as like as two peas in a pod!'

Twins.

Emma felt a shiver – of what? Shock? Recognition? Fear? – tingle down her back.

'Twins!' she whispered.

Harriet glanced up from her reading, a startled expression on her face. Then rising quickly she returned the magazine to the centre table and riffled through the pile, looking for one that was more interesting.

The outside door opened again and a heavily-built woman came in, with a dog on a lead.

'You don't mind, do you?' she asked, holding the lead towards the receptionist who was still speaking on the phone.

'Just a minute and I'll be with you Mrs Martineau,' the receptionist replied sounding harassed and continuing to speak into the telephone, taking down particulars.

The woman lowered herself into a chair opposite Harriet and Emma, breathing heavily and perspiring. Her dog, a cairn terrier as fat and as breathless as its mistress, sat at her feet and yawned.

'I know it's not the done thing,' the woman explained. 'But she whines so if I leave her in the car – and it's that hot out. . . .'

'Now, Mrs Martineau – this isn't the vet's, you know,' the receptionist said, replacing the telephone.

'I'd be ever so grateful. She gets that fussed if I leave her alone. . . .'

'Go on then, but you'll get me shot. Mind, you'll have to leave her out here while you go in to see the doctor. This isn't a vet's. . . .'

'Kindly!' the dog woman said, with a nod. 'Who's on, any road?'

'Rogers,' the receptionist replied.

The woman with the dog was now openly staring at Emma and Harriet, while continuing her conversation with the receptionist.

'Oh, I always get Rogers. Where's Ransom?'

'Taken Mrs Ransom back down to London.'

'That poor woman! You're the decorator from the Hall, aren't you?' she said, without pausing for breath.

Harriet looked up from her magazine and at the same moment Emma giggled.

'Yes!' Harriet replied and then looked down quickly, catching Emma's giggles.

'I thought that's who you were. How d'you like stopping there, then?'

'It's very nice,' Harriet said, still not looking up and having difficulty keeping her voice steady.

'I suppose so! If you like that sort of thing. Wouldn't do for me. Too big and gloomy. 'Course the Shawcrosses have a lot of visitors. . . . Not that they're often there themselves. . . .'

The door to the consulting room opened and the mother and baby came out.

'Now then, Joyce!' the woman with the dog said.

'Mrs Martineau, how're you keeping?'

'Not so dusty. I've come for my check-up. I have a heart condition,' she explained to Harriet and Emma then turning back to the woman with the baby she added, 'I'd not have bothered coming if I'd known Dr Ransom was away. . . .'

'You can go in now, Mrs Charrington.'

'You don't need to come, Mother,' Emma said, getting up and going to the door.

'I'd better be with you,' Harriet said, hurrying after her.

Once they were both in the passageway at the other side of the door they collapsed against the walls, giggling helplessly.

'I thought I was going to die,' Harriet gasped. 'The bit about wallpapering!'

'They've probably never heard of rag rolling up here, Mother!'

'I'll do you if you go on about rag rolling. There are other paint techniques, you know,' Harriet said. Then she added as they were both starting to laugh again. 'Come on, let's get this over,' and they went into the door marked *ROGERS*.

Dr Rogers was an elderly man. He wore little half glasses with golden rims. He was seated at his desk, staring out of the window when they came in. He listened in silence as Harriet explained that Emma had been having trouble with her breathing and that as a baby she had suffered from asthma. Then he told Emma to lift her T-shirt so that he could listen to her chest.

Emma pulled up the shirt, carefully managing to keep the tattoo covered. He first listened to her back. Then he turned her round and listened to her chest. All the time Emma kept her hand holding the T-shirt firmly clasped over the tattoo.

'Mmmh! It's a bit wheezy. Nothing too bad, I'd say. Cold on the chest.'

'It was terrible during the night, though,' Harriet insisted, not wanting it to appear as though they were wasting his time.

Dr Rogers looked at Emma closely through his half glasses.

'See your tongue,' he said and when she stuck it out he stared at it gravely. 'Mmmh!' he said again. Then he felt the glands behind her ears and on her neck. 'Nothing too serious,' he said. 'Lift your shirt again.'

138

Taken by surprise Emma pulled up her T-shirt and exposed the tattoo.

'What have we here?' the doctor asked, peering through his half glasses, his head tilted slightly to one side, giving him an amused, quizzical look. 'Mmmh! How long have you had this?'

'What is it?' Harriet asked.

'It's all right, Mother,' Emma said, turning her back on Harriet.

'That's for me to decide,' Dr Rogers said, his nose inches from her shoulder. 'Some sort of tattoo, is it?'

'Tattoo?' Harriet asked, surprised.

'Is it sore?' the doctor asked, pressing the skin.

'No,' Emma mumbled, trying not to wince.

'Em. What's this about?' her mother asked, moving round so that she could see the shoulder.

'Show your mother,' Dr Rogers said, drawing away in order to let Harriet have a better view.

'Who did this?' Harriet asked, her voice horrified.

'I did,' Emma replied.

'You?' Harriet cried. 'I thought we agreed that you would not have a tattoo until you were eighteen? Look at it! It's difficult to tell what it's supposed to be even.'

'It's a star,' Emma said, beginning to feel angry. She hated them both staring at her as if she were some sort of specimen under a microscope.

Dr Rogers now moved back in for a second look.

'A star is it? It's difficult to recognize as such. And you say you did it?'

'Yes,' Emma replied, staring at him defiantly.

'Mmmh! Well you're very lucky you didn't give yourself blood poisoning at the same time.' He took

139

out a pen and turned back to face his desk. 'I'll give you some expectorant for the cough. . . .'

'I haven't got one,' Emma said.

'Then you should have. Far better to get that phlegm off your chest.' He glanced at Harriet, as though hoping for a less surly reception from her than from her daughter. 'And five days of anti-biotics. Take the pills three times a day, with food.' As he spoke he was writing out a prescription. Then he stared at Emma again.

'When I was a young man, a group of us had tattoos done at a parlour in Whitby. Mine is a blue bird. On the upper arm. I have regretted it ever since. Though it has faded with the years, it is still there as a reminder of a foolish act; a foolish act of a foolish age. Come back if you don't feel any better.' And, rising, he walked over to the door and held it open for them both.

The receptionist told them that the prescription would be ready by early evening. As they were about to leave, Emma asked her if Tim Ransom was also away with his parents.

'Oh, you've met young Tim, have you? No, he's at home. His aunt is living with them at the moment. To help look after Mrs Ransom. You'll know she's not been at all well, do you? Dr Ransom's taken her down to the Marsden for treatment. This is her third visit. He says she's responding very well, but of course she looks terribly worn, poor woman.'

'Come on, Emma,' Harriet called from the door.

'Shall I give him a message – young Tim?'

'Only if you see him,' Emma said hurrying to the door.

'Well what do you want me to say?'

140

'Just that I was asking,' Emma replied.

All the way back in the car Harriet complained about the tattoo. But Emma wasn't really listening to her. She had other much more important things on her mind.

DIARY

Twins! Why didn't I think of it sooner? There are two of them. That's why they seemed to be at opposite sides of the room last night. Two boys looking identical. Except, come to think of it, one of them looks sad and as if he wants me to help him and the other was goading me and trying to frighten me and has a really evil gleam in his eyes!

Presumably most of this would be quite easy to verify. It must be part of the history of the place. If only Tim's mother wasn't away. He said she knew a lot about what went on here . . . including a murder. Something about a governess (who I've seen) and a little boy (ditto × 2!). Tim's mother has gone down to London to a hospital. Mother says it specially deals with cancer patients. I suppose I could ask Lynda if she knows about the twins who used to live here – but she doesn't seem very interested and her father (who could really help me) is dotty!!
WHAT I THINK I KNOW
I'm sure they were twins that I saw last night. It's the only way to explain how the same boy was in two places at once. IDENTICAL TWINS – only one of them is much more friendly than the other.

But that really doesn't explain how I was dreaming it all. I mean that suggests I've suddenly become clairvoyant. . . .

Which leads to a really FRIGHTENING THOUGHT – if it wasn't a dream (like the governess being dazzled by the spectacles was definitely a dream – I mean, I'm certain about that) then what does that tell me? That I'm being haunted? But if I'm being haunted – how come I was fighting with myself on the bed?? THAT bit had to be a dream . . . I can't be haunting myself! And besides – why should I be being haunted? What have I got to do with something that went on in this house (which I didn't even know existed until last week) and which happened ages ago anyway. . . . I mean – WHY IS THIS HAPPENING TO ME?? I'm a stranger here. . . .

Confusion is making my head ache. I'd better stop for a bit.

2

She could hear the noise the builders were making as though it was coming from the end of a long tunnel. The banging seemed to echo round the room, catching the rhythm of her heartbeat and adding to the throbbing pain in her head.

She lay on the bed and pulled the covers over her. She was still in the clothes that she had worn to go to see the doctor. Although the day was warm and sunny after the thunder, she felt cold inside and kept shivering.

She closed her eyes. The pillow was hot under her cheek . . .

A hand surrounded by a delicate lace cuff reached out to the bedside table. Another hand, with the same lace at the wrist, held a small bottle. The first hand picked up a piece of white cotton edged with lace. The second hand sprinkled the stuff from the bottle onto the material. Then the hand came back towards her, mopping her sweating forehead with the cool, damp handkerchief. The smell of lavender and roses was overpowering . . .

Emma woke with a start.

She was lying facing the open window. The noise of the builders was very loud. She felt hot and cold, awake and still asleep. The room around her was familiar and yet for a moment she couldn't recall where she was. Then she noticed the cloying, sweet smell of lavender and roses . . .

She rose from the bed. A sudden, unnatural silence had descended over the room. After all the noise there was something ominous about the stillness that surrounded her. She slipped a shawl over her shoulders and, with a racing heart, she crossed to the nursery stairs.

The door at the bottom was closed. She went down into the dark.

She saw the lower door being pushed open by the same delicate lace-cuffed hand.

The room was empty. The covers on the two narrow beds were pushed back as though their occupants had jumped out in a hurry.

The door leading to the landing was open. She crossed towards it, walking as if in slow motion.

The house was so quiet. Dappled light spilled from the long windows. She walked as far as the stairwell and looked down into the hall.

Behind her the sudden sound of a door banging made her swing round. At once another door, at the other side of the house, banged, making her turn quickly. As she did so the sound of racing feet echoed away behind her, disappearing in the direction of the nursery.

She turned once more and with determined tread retraced her steps to the nursery.

As the door drew closer, she could hear her heart beating so fast she thought it would burst.

The nursery appeared to be empty.

She went inside looking for whoever had run in, but she searched in vain. Her head was aching terribly now. Wearily she crossed back to the stairs intending to go up to her room.

The door at the top of the stairs was closed. She tried to open it. It was locked . . .

Sudden terrible panic. She must get back down to the bottom of the stairs before they locked that door as well. She turned and tripped, sprawling against the narrow walls, desperately trying to regain her balance, stumbling and losing control as she fell down the steep flight of stairs.

She landed on the floor half in and half out of the nursery door. Above and behind her she could hear uncontrolled, high giggling laughter.

The boy came slowly down the stairs towards her. He was laughing so much that he held his sides, his whole body shaking. She pulled away from him, staring at him with disbelief. He slowly raised an arm, his body shaking with laughter, and pointed a trembling, accusing finger at her. His face was convulsed with demonic glee. Then, very childlike, very small and young, he covered his face with his hands and danced round her.

She grabbed him as he passed her, catching the shoulder of his nightshirt. He tried to wriggle free but before he could manage to do so, her other hand had taken a fistful of his black hair. She was pulling it so that it made him cry out. With her other hand she started to beat him about the body, slapping and punching and overwhelmed with anger.

144

All she had wanted to do was to stop his laughter. Now, as his screaming grew louder and more uncontrolled, she could hear her own gasping sobs mingling with it into a cacophony of sound . . .

Appalled by what was happening – by her action, by the boy's behaviour, by the fear and loathing that they both shared for each other – she flung the boy into one of the beds and reeling backwards she sank down onto the top of a trunk-like wooden box, placed under the window.

The boy was whimpering now. But if she had looked closely and had not been consumed with her own guilt, her own despair, she would have seen that he watched her through the slits of his eyes and that his lips were curled in a delighted, malevolent grin.

Much later after he had fallen asleep she went in search of his brother. She knew he would be terrified, that he would be hiding somewhere, afraid to come out. She called for him from room to room. But she didn't find him.

3

'Oh, you're asleep are you?' Lynda Carver said, coming into the room. 'You've got a visitor.'

'A visitor?' Emma said, sitting up quickly, surprised by this sudden intrusion.

'Your boyfriend!' Lynda replied. 'I've left him downstairs. I didn't think it decent him coming up to your room – I wasn't sure what you might get up to!'

'Who is it, Lynda?' Emma asked, irritably.

'Well how many boyfriends do you have up here? Tim Ransom, of course.'

'Tim's here?' she asked, scrambling out of bed.

'Look at the sight of you, lying down fully clothed . . .'

'I'm not well.'

'Shall I tell him you're too poorly to see him, then?'

'No. No, I'm coming! I'm coming,' Emma called, grabbing her sponge bag and pushing past her on the way to the bathroom. 'I just have to make myself look beautiful!'

'Oh, I'll tell him to come back again in a few years' time, then,' Lynda said, straightening the bed as she spoke.

Tim was sitting in the kitchen when Emma came down.

'Hello,' he said rising with a smile as she came in from the back hall.

'Where's Lynda?'

'One of the men came – the builders. Evidently they've found an extra bit of room or something. They seemed quite excited. Your mother was here, having a cup of tea – they wanted her to see it.'

As he was speaking Emma felt an inexplicable shiver of fear. She looked over her shoulder, frowning.

'What did they mean, an extra bit of room?'

'Something about the panelling they're removing . . . Are you any better? I'm sorry, I didn't know you'd been ill till Dad's receptionist told me . . .'

But Emma wasn't really listening. She was already going towards the main part of the house. Something he had said had stirred strange memories deep in her psyche. She had to go and see.

'Come if you like,' she called over her shoulder,

her steps quickening as she started to run towards the hall doors. 'You said you've always wanted to see inside this place.'

With Tim in pursuit she went through the double doors into the main hall and up the stairs to the landing, following the now familiar route. It's as though I've always lived here, she thought, as she turned towards the corridor leading to where the builders were working. She felt as if she were physically retracing her recent steps. As if it wasn't a dream she'd just been having when Lynda came in . . . but reality, she thought. The idea was so unnerving that she gasped. How could such a reality exist?

'I'm being stupid,' she said, angry with herself.

'What did you say?' Tim asked, having to run to keep up with her.

Emma glanced at him, surprised. She had forgotten he was even there. She looked at him as if he were a stranger, less real than the small boy who only moments before had danced and mocked and pointed at her; the small boy whom, in her anger, she had wanted to hurt and beat and pummel into silence.

'Stephen!' a voice in her head shouted, its tone filled with anger and frustration.

'Stephen! Yes, that's right,' Emma whispered. 'His name is Stephen and . . . the other one is . . . Samuel.'

She stopped in her tracks outside the nursery door and turned to look at Tim – nice, real, very human Tim standing beside her, panting with the speed of the chase.

'How do I know that?' she whispered.

'Know what?'

She started to tremble, felt panic at the back of her throat, wanted to run away, to hide, not to go into the room.

'I'm frightened,' she gasped.

'It's OK,' he said, looking puzzled and reaching towards her. 'There's nothing to be frightened about.'

The nursery was crowded with people. All four of the builders were there as well as Lynda and Harriet. They were all standing facing the wall where the stairs leading to Emma's room ran steeply upwards. Now, no longer boxed in by wooden panelling, the stairs and the space under them had been revealed.

'Oh, there you are,' Harriet said as Emma came in followed by Tim.

'What's happened?' Emma heard a voice ask and then realized it was her own.

'This room has just grown by about three feet!' her mother said.

Tom, the builder with the long hair, looked over his shoulder at her and smiled.

'We thought, when we started to remove the panelling, we'd find solid wall behind. Wrong!'

'But these stairs were here before the Victorian panelling, surely?' Harriet said.

'Yeah, must have been,' Bill, the other builder said, inspecting the timber.

'What, you mean they were just open to the room – like they are now? That doesn't seem at all in keeping with the period.'

'No. The stairs would originally have been boxed in somehow. Yes – look! You can see the remains of lath and plaster here,' Bill continued. 'When they were doing the rooms up, they must have decided to replace this wall for some reason.'

'I don't understand what all the fuss is about,' Emma said, feeling a strange sense of anticlimax.

'We've just given your mother another headache, that's all!' Tom said.

'Thank you very much!' Harriet said, with a grim smile. 'You're going to have to box it all in again and then plaster over it. Damn – that means more delay. This is not turning out to be an easy job!'

'Sorry about that,' Bill said. 'If only it could have been an interesting find – like a medieval priest hole, or a secret hoard! Still, there is this old oak kist. Looks Jacobean to me.'

'Don't you think that's really odd, though? The way they walled it in behind the new panelling – as though they were hiding it, or had forgotten it was there?' Harriet remarked and as she spoke she moved forward, revealing for the first time to Emma's view a long, wooden, trunk-like box.

Emma gasped. She recognized it at once. It was the one on which she had rested after she and the boy had fought in this room only . . . moments before? Years ago? In a dream? In reality?

Then, as she watched, her mother reached forward and lifted the thick metal hasp and, using both her hands, she pulled open the top of the box.

For a moment the moving picture in front of Emma's eyes went still and all sound receded into throbbing silence. It was as if everyone in the room and even the room itself seemed to freeze, held still and mute in anticipation of some terrible event . . .

Then, from far far away a terrible, anguished, shattering scream echoed down the years, rending the fabric of the nightmare she was witnessing and shattering the image like broken, flying glass.

In slow motion Emma saw all the occupants of the room – her mother, Lynda Carver, each of the builders and lovely, real Tim – turn towards her. Some of them were reaching out to her, others drew back as if alarmed.

She felt hemmed in on all sides, squeezed and jostled by a crowd that pushed and vied for a better view. Unseen bodies, ghost bodies, streamed into the room, gathering around her where she stood near to the door. She could scarcely breathe for the volume of the crowd and the morbid fascination of the onlookers.

Her mother still held the box lid half open and then, with a single movement, she pushed it wide and turned to step towards Emma.

The scream grew and lengthened then gradually turned from the expression of terror into an endless sob of despair.

Emma brought her hands up to cover her ears, trying to blot out the awful sound and, as she did so, she turned and fought her way through the crush of bodies that surrounded her, pushing and shoving and forcing her way out of the room. At last, reaching the landing, she was relieved to feel more space around her and the air was fresh.

Without pausing, she turned and ran for her life.

Eight

1

The garden baked in the heat of the day. The shrubs in the long borders on either side of the lawn wilted under the probing, searching rays of the sun. Huge bushes of old roses, some so enlarged with age that they had to be supported by rough wooden props, leaned heavily towards low hedges of pale grey and mauve lavender that marked the edge of each of the formal beds.

'The scent is almost suffocating, isn't it?' Tim remarked.

Emma turned and stared at him, surprised.

He was lying on the lawn beside her while she sat with her legs drawn up, her arms encircling the knees.

'What did you say?' she asked.

'The scent,' he murmured, his eyes closed as if he were drifting off into sleep, 'it's so strong it's almost like an anaesthetic.'

'You can smell it too?' she gasped, relieved.

Tim opened his eyes and squinted up at her, holding a hand as a shade against the glare of the light.

'Of course I can.'

'What is it? Where's it coming from?'

'All around us,' he replied, sitting up and indicating the surrounding garden. 'Mainly the lavender and the roses, I should think.'

Puzzled. Emma turned and looked at the border across the lawn in front of them.

'Lavender and roses,' she said quietly. 'I suppose if my bedroom window is open all the time it's small wonder that the scent fills the room.'

'Sorry, you've lost me,' Tim said, leaning back and settling himself comfortably on the grass once more. 'I don't know what you're talking about.'

'Ghosts,' Emma replied, after a long pause.

'Ah, yes!' Tim said, with a contented sigh. 'Go on then – tell me about what's been happening.'

His voice was so matter of fact, the request so ordinary, that she found she was responding before she had time to stop herself. Quietly, without looking at him, she began to recite the chapter of events, the dreams and the hauntings and all the strange occurrences that had taken place since she and Harriet had come to Borthwick Hall.

Starting with the evening when they had arrived at the front gates and she'd seen the gleam of light from the Games Room window, she worked slowly and unemotionally through each of the happenings without hesitation. Not once did she have to pause or backtrack. Each occurrence presented itself in her mind from the store of her memory – the footsteps and the lights going off; the governess and the hand on the banister; the fight in the bed; the mocking laughter; the whispering; the banging doors; the boy at the window – she left nothing out.

Tim didn't interrupt her with any questions; didn't show any surprise; didn't even once check something she had just said, or ask her to clarify a point. She thought perhaps he had fallen asleep or that his mind had wandered and he wasn't listening to her any more. But it didn't matter. In a way she wasn't telling him, it was more as if she were talking to herself and she realized that she was finding the process strangely soothing. Somehow externalizing the events into this long monologue took the importance away from them. It was having much the same effect as light has on darkness or fresh air in a frowsty room; it was clearing the atmosphere, taming the extraordinary and taking away at least some of the fear.

Eventually she reached the incidents of the morning. The dream – for that was how she now designated it – of the confrontation with 'Stephen', as she now thought of the boy, when she or the governess or she as the governess had beaten him, tearing his hair by the handful, wanting to obliterate and destroy him. As she recreated the scene, she felt the strong surge of the emotion sweeping over her again, making her shake and gasp. For the first time her voice betrayed her inner turmoil. She described how she had thrown the child back onto his bed and then sunk down onto the wooden chest beside the window. She remembered precisely the feeling of shock and fear that had engulfed her, the desire to kill.

'And then when we went back there together . . . they were all standing, staring at that same chest. It had been hidden from view until that moment. No one knew it was there. No one could have told me about it. But I knew it was there. Can you understand what I'm saying? I knew it was there, Tim. I'd seen it before. It's such a pointless, unim-

153

portant thing to know. But I did, Tim. I really did. I'd seen that box before. And I wasn't making it up this time – because all of you were there looking at it with me. You were seeing it as well. All of you . . .' For a moment her courage failed her. She could feel again the unseen crowd, pressing in around her. Then shaking away the growing sense of fear she continued: 'But all it was was a wooden box. I mean, I could understand my reaction if they'd just unearthed a skeleton, or treasure trove or . . . She shook her head. 'But – just a measly old wooden box that was once used as a window seat. I suppose what got to me was that it confirms that I've been dreaming about – or experiencing, or whatever you like to call it – the past and I have to admit that that is pretty weird. But wouldn't you have thought it would reveal itself in a more significant way? I mean, when I finally know I'm being haunted – it's by a wooden box! It's like going through the whole of Hamlet and discovering that your particular ghost is a bit of the scenery!'

There was a long silence after she finished speaking. She could hear bees droning in amongst the roses and the distant singing of birds. Peaceful, country sounds. Again she thought that perhaps Tim was sleeping, that he hadn't heard any of her story. But then, in an ordinary voice, somewhere very close to her, she heard him speak for the first time since she had started her soliloquy and what he said shattered her world and sent her sliding towards terror.

'I suppose it's the box they found the body in,' he said.

154

Tim's mother had been ill for three years. Or rather it was three years since the cancer had finally been diagnosed. She had probably been suffering from the symptoms for a while before that without them having been noticed. During that time she had had a number of periods of remission when it had almost seemed that she was cured.

'. . . And we still think she will be – cured, I mean – it's just that sometimes when she comes back from treatment she's in such a bad way, so weak and sick, that I almost wish it could end, because I can't bear to see her going on suffering. I know that's selfish and I've never said it to anyone before but it's the truth . . .'

They were walking across the meadow towards the pond where they had first met. Tim had promised to tell Emma all he knew about the murder at Borthwick but now, instead, he was telling her about his mother's illness. Emma felt an unforgivable wave of irritation sweep over her, which she immediately stifled and then felt guilty about. But, honestly, she didn't want to know about his mother – she'd never even met the lady and, although she was very sorry that she was ill, it really had nothing at all to do with her.

'How does she know about the murder at Borthwick, anyway?' she asked and then immediately felt guilty again, for interrupting him.

'That's what I'm trying to explain,' Tim replied. 'It's because of her illness that she started to research local history. You see, she used to be always busy. But when she's on chemotherapy it leaves her feeling weak and tired. She decided she was beginning to vegetate – so she started to do the research to keep her mind active. In a way I think it's kept her alive. She's really got very interested in it all. She wants to do a book about it.'

As he walked he kept stooping forward and picking fronds of long grass which he wound into bundles round his fingers. Then he threw them up into the air and watched them fall gently to the ground. The heat of the day had turned sticky and humid again and the bright sun was shrouded behind a haze.

'So, go on then – what did she discover?' Emma prompted him.

Tim looked at her sideways, a puzzled expression on his face. It was as though he had forgotten what they were talking about.

'The murder, Tim!' Emma said, impatiently.

'Oh, yes! It was some time in the middle of the last century – between 1860 and 1870, I think. Round about then. I made notes . . .' And, as he spoke he took a few folded sheets of paper out of the back pocket of his jeans. 'That's why I came to see you . . .' He scanned the sheets, reminding himself of the facts. 'The family were called Westlake. They'd owned the Hall and most of the land round here for centuries. It was still Westlake property right up until the Shawcrosses took it over . . .'

'But it had been empty for a long time when they bought it,' Emma cut in, remembering what Lynda had told her.

'You already know all this?' Tim said, sounding disappointed.

'No, no. I don't know anything. Let's go under the trees . . .' and she ran on ahead into the cool shade of the wood.

When Tim reached her, Emma was sitting beside the pond near the willow where they had first met.

'You fancy going in for another swim then?' he asked as he approached. There was a grin in his voice that instantly irritated her.

'I haven't got a costume with me,' she said.

'That didn't stop you last time! I meant to ask you – is that a tattoo you have on your shoulder?'

'You said you didn't look,' she snapped, feeling embarrassed.

'I didn't. Well, only when you were down in the water – but I couldn't help seeing your shoulder.'

'Yes, it's a tattoo,' she said, staring at him defiantly. 'Now do you want to discuss my body or are you going to tell me about the murder?'

'I'd quite like to have a tattoo. . . .'

'TIM!' Emma yelled.

'What?'

'You're impossible. Either tell me what you came to tell me – or I'm going home.'

'No, please don't!' His voice sounded urgent and tinged with sadness.

'I'm waiting,' Emma said, not meeting his eyes because she could sense his unhappiness and she didn't know how to cope with it.

Tim cleared his throat and sat down on the grass at a little distance from her.

'There's not a lot, really. Apparently it was quite a famous case – so it wasn't difficult for Mum to research it. There was a governess, a Miss Grey. She was in charge of the two young sons of the household. . . .'

'One of them was called Stephen,' Emma said, stating fact without knowing for certain that she was correct.

'That's right. Stephen and Samuel. . . .'

'Samuel?' Emma repeated him, frowning, 'That was the name of old Mr Westlake who lived here at the end.'

Tim glanced at his notes.

'Yes. Samuel was the one who survived. He lived on here alone after his parents died, right into his old age.'

'So it was he who Lynda's father worked for as a young man.'

Tim shrugged.

'I suppose so, I don't know.'

'It must have been. How odd, I thought it was a much longer time ago. You think of the Victorian age as history – and yet there are people alive now who knew people who were alive then.' She shook her head, frowning and then shrugged. 'Sorry, I'm interrupting you – what happened to Stephen?'

'He was found dead in an oak chest in the nursery. He had suffocated. Miss Grey was charged with his murder. Apparently it happened when all the family apart from the young sons were out hunting.'

'Where was the other brother while this took place?'

'That all came out at the trial – which took place in York on. . . .'

'Where was he?' Emma repeated the question impatiently.

'It was two days before he was found. He had hidden behind a wardrobe in one of the top rooms . . . He was terrified. It was suggested at the trial that he had been lucky to have escaped with his life.'

'You mean – Miss Grey was going to murder him as well?'

Tim shrugged. 'That was the assumption.'

'What happened to her?'

'Miss Grey? That's the weird bit. She refused to have legal help. She put up no defence of her own. I think she sounds a bit mad. But that's just me, guessing.'

'I don't think she was in the least bit mad. Why do you say that?'

'She was up on a murder rap, right? She knew what the penalty would be if she was found guilty. Yet she didn't speak at the trial, other than to answer basic questions. She offered no explanations, no excuses for what had happened. In fact she more or less condemned herself by her behaviour. She set the jury against her by seeming not to care about the boy. If she'd been more concerned, the outcome could have been totally different. All the evidence was circumstantial. The only incriminating factor was that she was alone in the house with the two children at the time. But what took place could easily have been an accident. The child could have climbed into the chest – playing hide and seek . . . the latch could have slipped. He would have been trapped. It was during the day. There was no reason for anyone to have heard his screams if they weren't in the nursery . . . But none of this was even considered. The family accused Miss Grey and she . . . did nothing to defend herself.'

'What happened to her?' Emma asked. She felt cold in spite of the day and her heart was beating fast and too loud.

'She was found guilty,' Tim replied, 'and she was later hanged at York.'

'Poor woman,' Emma whispered.

'The Westlake family were absolutely shattered. It's said that they never recovered and that from that time the estate started to go downhill and the house fell into disrepair. A lot of the servants left – maybe they were dismissed, or maybe they didn't want to stay any longer. And the family, Mr and Mrs Westlake and their remaining son, Samuel, became more or less recluses. That's it really. That's all the notes I made. The family tombs are at the church by the way . . .'

'I'll go and look sometime,' Emma said, her mind miles away, deep in other thoughts.

'When we went into that room,' Tim continued, 'and they were all looking at the wooden chest . . .' He shook his head, remembering. 'I mean, it's so obvious, isn't it? That was the chest it happened in. They must have hidden it away . . . I suppose they didn't know what else to do with it. . . .'

'You'd think they'd have burnt it. I wouldn't want something like that stuck away behind the panelling. No wonder there are ghosts there.'

'You really believe that?'

'What? That I'm being haunted? There's no question. I've told you what's been happening.'

Tim nodded, thoughtfully, then he frowned and looked at Emma.

'Why you, though? You're only a visitor. I mean the Shawcrosses live here – do they get haunted? And all their guests? They have a stream of visitors . . . Have any of them been haunted?'

'I don't know,' Emma replied, trying to focus her attention on his words. 'It's maybe partly the room I'm sleeping in.'

'Which room?'

'I'm in Miss Grey's room,' as she used the name she felt a shiver of excitement, 'the one immediately above the nursery. But it's used as a guest room now – so I can't be the first person who's slept in it.'

'What about Lynda Carver? Has she seen anything?'

'No. I'm not sure she even believes in it all. She refers to it as one of her father's stories.' Then, without pausing, she changed the subject as a new thought occurred to her. 'Maybe she was covering up for someone else.'

'Sorry?' Tim asked, confused.

'Miss Grey, at her trial.'

'How d'you mean?'

Emma turned and stared at Tim, but she didn't answer his question. Half-formed imaginings – or were they memories? – were crowding into her mind. She needed time before she could express them.

'Did your mother mention that they were twins?' she asked instead.

'Um, I don't think so,' Tim said and then, without any warning and totally taking her by surprise, he started to cry.

'What's the matter?' Emma asked, after staring at him in disbelief for a moment.

The boy just shook his head and turned away from her. He was sitting on the grass cross-legged and now, with his back towards her, she saw his whole body shaking as volumes of stored up silent grief escaped from him.

Emma turned her head away. She was embarrassed by this show of emotion. She felt something

161

was expected of her – that she should do something to help him – but she didn't know what.

At last, after what seemed a long time, Tim reached into the pocket of his jeans and produced a handkerchief. With it he blew his nose noisily.

'Sorry!' he said, still keeping his back towards her.

'It's all right,' Emma mumbled.

'I didn't mean to do that . . . It was you mentioning Mother.'

'Did I?'

Tim blew his nose again and then stuffed the handkerchief back into his pocket.

'Dad says she will get better.'

'That's all right then.'

'But I think he just says it to cheer me up.' He turned and looked over his shoulder at her. 'Tell me things – go on, anything.'

He looked so desperate that Emma wanted somehow to help him. She felt a sudden overwhelming sadness – his sadness. She wanted to reach out to him, to touch him, to be gentle and reassuring with him.

'I expect she will get better,' she said.

Tim cleared his throat. 'Twins? No, she didn't mention that.'

'They are though,' Emma said emphatically. Then she smiled, realizing that she'd spoken of them in the present. 'Funny thing that – Lynda Carver's father is a twin as well.'

'Yes.' Tim said, sounding more cheerful. 'He's Georgie and his brother is Jack. Georgie used to do gardening for us before he got too old.'

'You mean dotty.'

162

Tim shrugged. 'He's just a bit forgetful, that's all.'

'Lynda says he's dotty.'

'He's all right. I like Georgie.'

'But it is odd, isn't it?'

'What?'

'Well, two sets of twins – I mean it isn't very usual.'

'I don't think they're all that rare,' Tim said.

'I'd hate it,' Emma said, with sudden feeling. 'Imagine having to share everything with another half!'

'Like marriage!' Tim smiled.

'No, much worse than that. Marriage is someone you choose. All right, you might go off them later, but you're never really connected to them. But a twin! Are you an only child?'

Tim nodded and looked sad again, so Emma hurried on, afraid that he might start crying.

'I used to think it would be great to have a brother or a sister . . . Funny thing is, I do have a couple of half-brothers and a half-sister – but I've never even met them, so they don't count. But I mean a sister of my own. I always did think it'd be a sister. But a twin sister! That would be horrible.'

'Why?'

'Because you'd never feel original. There'd always be another you in competition with you. I'd really hate that. I find it quite hard enough coping with myself without having to worry about someone else . . .' Then she stopped talking as another thought occurred to her. 'Just supposing that's what happened.'

'What?'

163

'That's it, Tim!' Emma said, suddenly rising up onto her knees. 'That's it.'

'What is?'

'One of them always looks as if he's crying out for help . . . the other is always doing mean, horrible things. What if the nice one . . . couldn't bear it any longer?'

'And?'

'If he . . . got rid of his brother.'

'You mean one twin killed the other?' Tim's voice was full of doubt.

'Why not?'

'No! It's too melodramatic. Things like that don't happen.'

'You were prepared to believe that the governess killed him.'

'Because that's far more likely.'

'Why?'

'They were only children.'

'So?'

'Children don't do that sort of thing . . . Or very rarely. Anyway, it's much more likely as I said earlier that it was an accident and not murder at all.'

'But, in that case, why didn't she defend herself?'

'I don't know,' Tim sounded irritable now. 'I wasn't there.'

'Yes, of course you're right,' Emma suddenly, and too quickly, agreed. 'It was probably an accident.' But she only said it to end the conversation. In her heart and in her head she was beginning to see things quite differently.

DIARY

Supposing . . .

*Stephen was the evil twin: Samuel was the good one.
Good – but maybe also a bit wet. Always running to
Miss Grey for protection. A goody-goody. Now that could
really drive a person to murder! In fact – maybe the good
one is quite as much to blame as the bad one. Maybe it
was the good one's goodness that drove the bad one to
behave badly? Or maybe they both hated each other and
tormented each other in their own ways? That sounds even
more likely. Yes! I don't think one was good and the other
bad . . . It doesn't work like that – any more than I am
all one thing or the other . . . We're a mixture. That's
why having a twin would be so impossible – they'd always
be showing you the other side of yourself. Being goody
when you're being vile . . . being vile when you are all
sweetness and light! If I'd had a twin sister I think I'd
have got rid of her years ago! I can imagine her really
bugging me. Or – would I have loved her?*

*WOULD I HAVE LOVED HER?? Another me to
talk to, to share with, to whisper to.*

Emma stopped writing for a moment and shook her
head. The voice was back, whispering and taunting
her . . .

'Little Emmy! Want a twinsy-winsy sister,
Emmy? Poor little Emmy?'

'Shut up!' Emma shouted. 'Just shut up!' and she
started to write again:

*Maybe a twin would have understood me and would have
helped me to understand myself? And I'd have had her to
understand as well . . . And to care for? Why not? Maybe
I'd really have liked her and cared about her.*

165

When Tim cried I didn't know what to do because I don't know how to 'care'. I'm not even sure what it means.

The only person I'm really close to is Mum – and we just row all the time. But sometimes I feel I want to care about her.

Come to think of it – does she care about me? I suppose so – but in a dutiful sort of way. Because Dad left her when I was born I've been her responsibility ever since. I expect she rather resents me but she doesn't allow herself to admit it.

He wanted her to get rid of me. That's what I haven't faced up to since she told me. He wanted her to get rid of me. I was in his way. I wasn't good for his career.

Well – I can see what he meant. It – I – was very bad timing! But I'm not going to let this turn into some major trauma for me. As I've never known him – NOT EVER – I'm certainly not going to get my briefs in a bind over it now.

BUT MOTHER. . . . now that's an altogether different thing. What did my arrival do to her?? It broke up her marriage, that's what. He went off to find fame and fortune and she was left holding the baby . . .

Which is all a long way from the 'Borthwick Ghosts', Emmy dear.

WHY DID I JUST CALL MYSELF THAT??? I hate the name 'Emmy' – that's what the voice calls me. Don't tell me it's starting to write for me now as well!!

Emma threw her biro down onto the page and got up and walked over to the window.

The memory of her voice made her suddenly nervous. She had grown accustomed to it over the years. Although she didn't like it, it didn't usually frighten her. But now, as she remembered it, she

166

felt as though she was being watched. Recently, since she had been here at Borthwick, she had heard the voice outside her head and in one of the dreams she had ended up fighting with herself.

She turned her back to the window, facing the room, half expecting to see herself sitting on the bed watching her.

Involuntarily her hand reached up to her shoulder, touching the place where she had given herself the tattoo. She crossed quickly to the mirror on the dressing table and, pulling back her T-shirt, she looked at the little irregular black star, still rimmed with angry red blotches on the skin.

Then she smiled at her reflection in the mirror. For the first time since she had made it, the tattoo gave her the sort of comfort which she had expected.

It was her distinguishing mark. While it was there on her shoulder she would know who she was. It gave her courage, confidence, an identity.

'This is me,' she whispered, pointing at the star. 'I am Emma.'

Nine

1

A door slammed, the sound cutting through the silence of the house.

It was the middle of the evening. Harriet was down in the small sitting room watching television. There was no one else in the house. There was no breeze. There was no reason for the door to slam.

It was beginning again.

Emma crossed and stood in her open doorway, looking along the shadowy corridor.

It's beginning again, she thought.

She felt calm – and as cold as ice. In a way she almost welcomed the fact that the haunting was starting again. She had known it would eventually and the anticipation had been unsettling her, making her restless and nervy. Now, at once, she was ready.

And besides these events from the past have nothing to do with me, she thought, so I have nothing to fear from them. I'm just a spectator – chosen for some reason to witness what really happened and maybe eventually to tell the truth about it all. Maybe in some strange way I'm connected to Miss Grey and it's her story I have to put right. Maybe when I came to stay in her room she recognized something about me that was sympathetic to her cause. Maybe she realized that we were close. I do feel close to her cause. Maybe we share characteristics – perhaps she never knew her father, like I've never known mine. Or, I don't know, maybe we have the same birth sign or a similar DNA or . . . I don't know. I don't know! I'm no good at knowing reasons, I don't need explanations, I'm prepared just to allow things to happen. Maybe Miss Grey took one look at me and decided she liked me. Maybe she knew at once that I'd believe in her and she was relieved because that's what she's been wanting all along – someone to believe in her . . .

'Hello?' she called, but not loudly and certainly not expecting any answer.

All the doors were closed except for her own. The only light came from the small window at the end of the corridor and from her bedroom.

She started to walk slowly along the passage in the direction of the back stairs. She didn't feel scared although with each step that she took away from the light she was aware of a growing heightened awareness – as though she were a radio being tuned to a high and elusive frequency or a pair of binoculars gradually being squeezed into sharper focus on a distant view.

She was about halfway along the corridor when a draught of warm air redolent with the heady sweetness of roses and lavender swirled in around her.

It's from the garden, she thought as her steps faltered and she had to fight for breath. My window is open. It's a perfectly ordinary thing that's happening. I am smelling the garden. It's evening, that's when the scents are at their most potent. There is nothing extraordinary about it. It's not Miss Grey's perfume . . . it's from the plants in the garden.

'Samuel?' someone called from a place very near to her. It didn't surprise her. It seemed quite natural. It was not a loud voice, not an urgent call, but a soft and gentle invitation to reveal oneself. 'Samuel, where are you, dear?' the voice murmured on the scented air.

Still Emma remained calm and detached. Whatever was happening could perhaps be explained as being in her imagination. But even if she accepted that she was being haunted it wasn't a very frightening experience because what was happening had nothing to do with her personally. She was simply a bystander. In some strange way she had stumbled on a series of events from the past that were locked into the house and had never been released.

It was as if a loud noise, caught in a drum, was echoing and reverberating once the lid had been lifted, she told herself; or the scent of old leather, waiting over the centuries was only now being smelt; or brandy, bottled years before, having lingered, waiting for someone to draw the cork, was at last being tasted.

Comforted by reason, Emma continued to walk slowly towards the end of the landing. Then she noticed that the door to one of the rooms facing the front of the house was standing slightly ajar.

There is nothing peculiar about this, she told herself. One of the doors isn't quite closed, that's all. It's trivial and unimportant.

170

Very slowly the door swung open and, as she turned towards it, she was able to see inside.

It was an ordinary, square, low ceilinged room, almost identical to the one she was using. It had two beds, a wardrobe with a mirrored front, a dressing table, a chest of drawers, an armchair, table, lamps . . . All this she took in at a glance, although later she would also remember that there was not much light showing through the heavily curtained window and that therefore it was surprising that she had seen so many of the details.

At first she naturally thought the room was empty but then, perhaps as her eyes grew accustomed to the gloom, she became aware of a figure sitting on one of the beds.

Whoever it was appeared as no more than an indistinct shadow with its back turned towards her. The person seemed so quiet and contained that Emma didn't like to intrude upon him or her.

'Samuel!' the call came again. It was so close to her that it felt like her own voice. It was the sort of sound she would make if she were about to play a trick and was luring someone into her trap.

From somewhere behind her came the sound of a high, giggling laugh. It was so sudden that it took her unaware, making her start with surprise.

'Samuel!' the voice called again, more urgently.

Then, with a rush of cold air, footsteps passed so close to her that she almost believed that she felt something bump against her shoulder. She turned quickly and saw a shadow disappearing through the open door of her own room.

At almost the same moment a strange, at first unidentifiable sound made her spin round again. It was so nearly human yet she recognized it as an animal cry; a yelp of protest, of pain, of shock. As she turned she saw the figure on the bed spring up and run towards and past her, knocking her sideways as it pushed its way out of the room.

Emma turned once more with the racing figure and glimpsed a familiar face. But everything was happening so quickly that she didn't have time to order her thoughts, to make sense of the impossible. The face she had seen . . . the person running away from her . . . looked like. . . .

'ME!' she gasped. 'It was me!'

Her breathing became tight as though there was a thick band tied tightly round her chest, preventing her from filling her lungs. The awful bubbling sound of phlegm filled the room with its moist, damp wheezing. Emma lurched forward, clutching at her throat, pulling the loose neck of her T-shirt down as though in some way it was choking her. Panic was rising in her now. Her cool detachment had disappeared. Her heart was beating very fast. Her breathing was becoming more and more shallow. She was gasping for air and she felt as if she were suffocating.

Emma staggered towards the bed, trying to calm herself, to force herself to breathe normally . . . to breathe in . . . to breathe out . . . to breathe in . . .

The cat, when she finally saw it, was curled up on the bed, purring and staring at her with those thin slits of eyes that seem to bore deep into your brain.

She crossed lethargically and sank down onto the bed beside it. The cat stretched and purred noisily. Emma leant towards it and gathered it up into her arms. It felt warm and its fur was like silk. It rubbed itself against her bare arms, purring and dribbling.

Emma could feel the skin on her arms itching and her breathing, although now under control, was restricted and wheezing. She knew it was the cat that was causing her this discomfort but she continued to hold it close, stroking it and feeling the thin body responding to her, as it purred and rubbed its face against her hand, biting her fingers gently with its sharp little teeth.

'Poor Beerbohm,' she whispered. 'It's all right. It's all right now. I'm sorry. I'm so sorry.'

2

Harriet was speaking on the telephone when Emma came in. She was laughing at something the person at the other end of the line had just said. She seemed very happy and relaxed. Because she had her back to the door, Emma was well into the room before she was aware of her presence.

'Here's Emma now,' Harriet said, looking round, and then a little too hurriedly she added, 'so, we'll hope to see you tomorrow evening, OK? Bye.'

She put the phone down guiltily and then turned towards Emma with a look of surprise.

'Darling! Where did that come from?'

The cat was cradled in Emma's arms and was purring loudly.

'I found it in one of the rooms on our landing.'

'Damn! I forgot all about it. The builders said they'd seen a cat in the yard yesterday. They asked Lynda if it belonged here. It doesn't. It's probably a stray. It'll have got into the house during the day. With this hot weather there've been doors open all the time. You'd better not hold it, darling. Give it to me. Listen to your chest! You've started wheezing again. . . .'

Harriet knew she was burbling. It was a way of covering up her embarrassment for having been caught on the phone talking to Simon. Not that she didn't have every right to speak to anyone she chose. But she didn't want yet another row with Emma. They'd been having too many recently and although usually they were both equally respons-ible, she always blamed herself. In some ways she realized that she was actually afraid of Emma. She would go to great lengths to avoid a confrontation with her.

Now, hoping that the matter was settled, she reached towards her daughter, intending to take the cat out of her arms. But Emma drew away, cower-ing back from her as if she were protecting both the animal and herself from some danger; as if she thought Harriet was about to attack them.

'No!' she screamed. 'Don't touch us.'

'Darling!' Harriet exclaimed. 'What is the matter with you.'

'Leave us alone,' Emma said, her whole body beginning to shake.

'Em! You're allergic to cats.' Harriet told her, still reaching towards her with her hands. 'Now give it to me. Look at your face and arms – covered in spots! That's the sign of an allergy. Listen to your breathing! It's making you ill again. Come on, give the cat to me.'

'If you take it – what will you do with it this time?'

'Put it outside!' Harriet said, in an ominously patient voice. 'It doesn't belong in the house anyway.'

174

'Get rid of it? Is that what you're saying? Like you did the last one?'

'Emma – the cat doesn't belong here.' Harriet's voice was taking on a dangerous note. 'And this isn't our house so even if we wanted to we can't just bring in any stray that happens along. Now I want you to take it out and put it in the yard. It can either find its own way home or it can take up refuge in one of the outhouses.'

'I won't.'

'Emma – do as you're told. Please. It's for your own good.'

'Yes, MY good!' she cried, rounding on Harriet furiously. 'It may be for my good. But what about Beerbohm's good? Mmmh? What about him?'

'Emma, that cat is not Beerbohm. Beerbohm has been dead for almost fifteen years . . .'

'I do know how old I am, Mother. And if I know that, I also know how long ago it is since Beerbohm was murdered.'

'Oh, heavens, child! You hadn't even heard about the stupid cat until I told you. You didn't even know it existed. Now give it to me and stop being such a pain!' And Harriet made a grab for the animal, pulling it out of Emma's arms.

The cat, taken by surprise, reared up, spitting angrily and clawing the air with its front paws. Holding it at arm's length Harriet walked with it out of the room.

'You can't simply kill things if they're inconvenient for you Mother!' Emma yelled after her. Then, when there was no answer, she ran out into the passage.

Ahead of her, Harriet was walking resolutely towards the back door. The cat, still dangling from her outstretched hands, was screaming and protesting loudly.

'Mother!' Emma shouted. 'You mustn't do this.'

Harriet had almost reached the back door. It was closed and in order to open it she would have to free one of her hands from their hold round the body of the cat.

She pushed the animal under one arm and was grappling with the heavy knob when Emma threw herself at her from behind.

'Emma!' Harriet screamed, trying to dodge away.

But Emma was convulsed with anger. She grabbed hold of her mother's hair and was trying to pull her round to face her. At the same time, with her other hand she was raining blows on Harriet's body. Somewhere in the back of her mind, even as this was happening, she was aware that she had acted like it before, or if not her then someone else, someone close to her, someone . . . Her anger was overwhelming, it gave her terrible strength.

'Give it to me! Give it to me! Give it to me!' she shouted over and over again as she lashed and pummelled with one fist while she pulled at the hair with the other.

Harriet meanwhile had managed to pull the door open. Fresh night air blew in from the yard.

As she tried to release the cat Emma dragged her sideways, striking her repeatedly.

The animal, terrified, scratched its way up Harriet's body, its stiletto sharp claws puncturing the skin of her upper arm, drawing bright specks of blood. Reaching her shoulder it turned its wild eyes on Emma. With a frightened screech it lashed out at her, ripping its claw across her cheek. As Emma flinched back, raising her hand to protect her eyes,

176

the cat dropped to the ground and streaked out of the back door into the safety of the night.

'Let go of my hair, Emma!' Harriet gasped.

With a sob Emma pushed her mother away from her and backed into the hall. Reaching the foot of the stairs she grabbed hold of the banister rail and using it as a lever she hauled herself upwards towards the top landing, taking the steps two and sometimes three at a time. She didn't stop running until she reached the bedroom corridor. Behind her she could hear her mother's footsteps, running up the stairs in pursuit.

She slammed the staircase door, giving herself valuable time, and ran along the corridor towards her room. Once inside she closed the door and leaned against it, panting for breath, her heart pounding, her head throbbing.

'Open this door at once, Emma!' she heard Harriet demand and she could feel the door moving behind her back as her mother pushed at it.

Taking a big breath to steady her nerves, Emma walked away from the door. Her weight being suddenly removed allowed the door to fly open under the pressure that Harriet was exerting on it from the other side. Her mother ricocheted into the room with such speed that she bumped into Emma and they both fell heavily, sprawling on the floor beside the bed.

In the silence that followed an owl could be heard screeching out in the dark world beyond the window. A slight breeze was blowing, freshening the atmosphere. Trees rustled gently. The curtains flapped.

'I'm sorry,' Emma whispered.

'Sorry! You were like a thing possessed!'

Emma began to cry quietly and after a moment Harriet crawled across the floor to her and put her arms around her, cradling her gently. Then they continued to sit on the floor in silence, listening to the distant night.

After a little while Emma heard Harriet giggle.

'Mother would have a fit!' she whispered.

'Your mother?'

'And *your* grandmother. She is a great upholder of civilized behaviour!'

'I'm sorry. It was my fault,' Emma whispered.

'Yes,' Harriet said after a moment, 'I can honestly say that this time I think it was.'

Emma felt terribly tired. The breath wheezed in her chest. Her cheek stung where the cat had scratched it. Beside her, Harriet settled with her back leaning against the side of the bed. Her arms were still round Emma so this movement pulled her back as well. She ended up leaning against her mother, both of them facing the door to the corridor, with their backs to the window.

'D'you want to get up?' Emma asked after a little while.

'No!' Harriet replied, dreamily. 'Let's just sit!' As she spoke she held Emma more firmly. 'I wanted to tell you something anyway. But you must promise to let me finish and not fly off the handle. Will you do that?'

'Fly off the handle? You know me. I can be guaranteed to lose my temper. . . .'

'No. Be serious, Em. Please. This is important to me.'

'Then it's bound to be about Simon Wentworth.'

'Don't say his name like that. . . .'

'Like what?' Emma protested.

178

'Please, Em!' Harriet pleaded with her. Then they both fell silent again.

'You want to marry him.' Emma said at last, making a simple statement and trying not to prejudice it with emotion.

'Yes,' her mother replied quietly.

'And he wants it as well?'

'He's the one that did the asking.'

'How very conventional, Mother dear! You of course said yes?'

'I told him I couldn't do anything without consulting you,' Harriet replied.

'He's not marrying me, Mother!' Emma quipped, trying to lighten the atmosphere with a joke.

'He is in a way,' Harriet countered. 'He'll be your stepfather. He'll be living with us.'

'In Talliser Road?' Emma asked, trying to imagine another person – anybody – fitting into the confined space of the little house.

'I suppose we'd move. He'd sell his flat, we'd sell the house. We could buy somewhere bigger with both lots of money.'

'It'd have to be near the river,' Emma said. 'I don't want to be dragged up to boring Hampstead or the desert wastes of Maida Vale.'

'I want to be married again, Emma,' Harriet said quietly. 'I was twenty-three when I last had a man in the house. . . .'

'You've had lots of boyfriends. Muti and I have lost count of how many.'

'Em, please! This is important to me. I'm talking about marriage, sharing life. Living with someone, being happy and unhappy in their company. Reading the Sunday newspapers in the same room, having rows and making up. Being a family – us,

179

the three of us. Going on holidays all together. Him getting to know you as well as he knows me . . .'

'I don't have to sleep with him, do I?'

There was a moment's silence then Harriet moved impatiently, releasing Emma. Getting up, she crossed to the window and leaned against the sill, looking out.

'You're not going to let it happen, are you?' she said, quietly.

Emma, still on the floor, rested her arms on the surface of the bed and looked at her mother.

'Can I meet him first?' she asked.

Harriet turned towards her.

'Poor Simon! It's not unlike applying for a job. What are your criteria for a suitable stepfather?'

'Having met him at least once.'

'You have. We all went – .'

' – To *Spartacus* together. You keep reminding me. But at the time I didn't know he was going to be using the bathroom every time I wanted to get into it. I didn't know we were going to be cosy in the Dordogne together. I didn't know he was going to teach me to drive and was going to buy me my first Porsche!' The two women looked at each other for a lingering moment and then Emma smiled. 'I'm too old for a pony.'

'He wants us to have dinner tomorrow night. He wants to ask you himself.'

'Oh, Mother! It's going to be terribly embarrassing!'

'Yes. But he'll be in a much worse state than you.'

Emma got up from the floor and walked slowly round the bed. She crossed to the dressing table and picked up her hairbrush. Then she sat on the stool and stared at herself in the mirror. The scratch on her cheek was thin and red and crusted with tiny beads of dry blood. Without really thinking about it, she started to brush her hair.

'Who's going to tell Muti?' she asked.

'You, I hope!' Harriet replied, with a smile.

'You're scared of your mother, aren't you?'

'Very.'

'She's all right, really,' Emma said, putting down the hairbrush but continuing to stare at her reflection. 'And what about Stephen?' she asked.

'What d'you mean?' Harriet sounded surprised by the question.

'Will you be telling him you're getting married?'

'Good God, no! Why would I? We haven't been in touch except through a solicitor since the night you were born.'

'Was that the night he left?'

'You could say that, yes.'

The face in the mirror stared out at her. Then it raised an eyebrow as though quizzically amused by what it saw. Emma turned her back and looked instead at her mother.

'What happened that night?' she asked.

Harriet sighed. The moment she had always known would one day have to be faced had come. But now that it had arrived what was hardest was not the telling but forcing herself to look back and remember.

'Stephen and I had a fight,' she said, speaking slowly, to stop her voice from shaking. 'Or rather we had an argument that grew into a fight. I was huge. It was hot, I remember, like it is now. The flat we had in St George's Drive was a basement. The air never seemed to reach it at the best of times.

Stephen had been to costume fittings that day. We hadn't been talking for weeks – months really. I suppose, looking back, that I was being rather unreasonable. No, I wasn't. He behaved like a pig. Or like a man. He felt no responsibility for the pregnancy at all. I was the one who was pregnant. Never once did he think that it might be on account of both of us. He just went ahead and got on with his life while I grew big and bloated and did all the right things at the clinic. That evening when he came in he'd been drinking with . . . I can't remember who now. Someone else on the film, I expect. He was on such a high. It WAS after all his big break. He was being treated like a star. Costume fittings, photographs, publicity. He was even being flown club class to the States. I resented every moment of it. I couldn't help it. I just hated him having such a good time and not bothering about me. I was low – scared even – and he was swanning around on a gigantic ego trip. That evening I'd had enough. There wasn't supper waiting for him nor a dutiful little wife. There was just me, eight and a half months pregnant, caged in a basement in the middle of a heatwave.' She paused and when she next spoke her voice was flat and dejected. 'He'd been drinking – and I was raring for a row. It was me. I started it. I kept it going. It was all my doing.'

'It's all right,' Emma cut in, 'you don't need to tell me any more.' She couldn't bear to see what the remembering was doing to Harriet. Her mother's expression was desolate, her eyes focused on that long-gone scene, her body tense, her arms folded across her breasts, her hands clenched.

But she seemed not to have heard Emma. Or if she had, she ignored her words.

'From the moment he came through the door,' she continued, 'I was shouting and within half an hour he was packing his bags. He must have had it all planned weeks before. Roger Aston let him stay until he flew off to LA and Roger hated having his life disrupted unexpectedly. He was a terrible old maid, though I loved him. That was the worst thing. I lost so many good friends. They were Stephen's originally, you see. People find it extraordinarily difficult to maintain both sides of a relationship after a split up.'

'So that was it? He just walked out?' Emma said.

'More or less it,' Harriet replied grimly. 'Unfortunately I goaded him so much that he swung a punch at me.'

'He hit you?' Emma asked incredulously.

Harriet smiled. 'Yes, he hit me. And I grabbed hold of him and hit him back.'

'People shouldn't behave like that,' Emma exclaimed.

'Excuse me!' Harriet said, smiling now. 'Isn't that a case of the pot and the kettle? I'm sure I shall have bruises from your recent attack!' Then she frowned. 'Maybe it's true, I am a born victim. I was told that once. Anyway, there was a nasty little fight – which I assure you was quite as much of my making as his – and he stumped out into the August night. About an hour later, thanks no doubt to the drama of it all, my waters broke . . . I was rushed to hospital. Muti, who was giving a dinner party at Strand-on-the-Green at the time, left her guests at the table . . . Imagine that! . . . in order to be with me. And after a lot of pushing and shoving and a few decidedly scary moments,' she threw wide

183

her arms and stepped forward like a music-hall comic, 'YOU!'

'But you did tell him I'd arrived, didn't you?'

'Yes, of course,' Harriet replied, briskly. 'We had a job finding him, but Muti was on the scent. When she finally tracked him down, some time the following morning, she no doubt gave him an ear full.'

'So he did see me?'

'He held you in his arms and I'm not at all sure that he didn't cry a little. And then he went to LA and became a superstar! Let's go downstairs and have a drink.' She held out a hand and when Emma took hold of it she pulled her up. 'We ought to put some TCP on that scratch as well.'

As they were walking back along the corridor towards the stairs Emma said: 'So we'll go out to dinner tomorrow night then and Simon – it's a ghastly name, Mother! Simon! As in "Simple Simon"! – anyway, HE can ask me for your hand in marriage!'

DIARY

Late – very late.

Mum and I have been talking and meanwhile she's had an awful lot of the Shawcross gin. (We'll have to buy them some more before we leave – and hide the empty bottles from Lynda C. who already disapproves of us without her adding severe alcoholism to the score). I think Mum feels guilty – and that she always has. (Not about drinking the Shawcrosses' gin!) I think she thinks it was her fault that she and Dad split up. That's why she's never been able to form another relationship with anyone – at least, not a lasting one. Though she has tried often enough. Now she wants to give it a go – with Simon –

and she's dead scared about it. Honestly! I've always lived in the belief that my elders were also supposed to be my betters! Tonight I spent most of the time reassuring my mother that everything was going to work out fine. Me! I did – and I am not yet fifteen! Nearly, but not quite. One thing is for sure, it's put me right off the idea of ever having a relationship myself. Should anyone come along who is prepared to take that risk they will find the door bolted and barred.

Anyway, we're going to have dinner with the adorable Simon (I must TRY to like him) tomorrow night and now I'm so tired that I'm going to sleep and it's no use any of the spooks trying to get me because they'll find I am dead to the world.

Ooops! I could have chosen a better expression than that! If I'm dead to the world – I'll have joined them. Oh well . . .

Ten

1

Dark. Warmth. A feeling, followed by movement. Slow motion. An arm stretching outwards and a body gradually turning.

Swimming in black water, the temperature of blood.

Distant sound. A bubbling, endless chord vibrating on the edge of the world.

Heaviness. A form, pressing the limit of the world inwards, confining space, diminishing territory.

A hand, small and crab-like, clenched then moving, fingers stretching. Legs entwined, kicking against the tepid, cloying fluid.

Another hand, reaching out; delicately feeling, palm against palm. A third hand, fingers probing, joining the discovery of the sensation of touch. One hand held within two hands; knuckle to palm, palm to palm. Praying hands, playing hands, touching, feeling, exploring,

A fourth hand – now there's a thing!

Two bodies, identifiable now. Two heads, four arms, four legs, two trunks, moving together in a measured, floating dance.

A single mind wanting to escape from the undulating motion of the blood-warm, restless sea.

The distant crash of unknown, unseen, not yet experienced wood against wood, as a door slams.

Voices raised in another world.

'Where've you been?'

'Out.'

'You're drunk!'

'Yes! And happy! And you can't bear either, can you?'

Sudden movement.

The beginning of the end of the world.

Emma woke to find she was hugging the pillow. Somehow she must have pulled it down in her sleep. She was lying with her arms wrapped round it, like a child holds a doll, for comfort maybe or perhaps for company.

The room was warm and she'd thrown the sheet off. But the breeze through the window had a keen edge, making her hot and cold at the same time.

Drowsily she pushed the pillow back under her head and pulled the sheet up from the end of the bed. She wrapped herself closely in it, as though wanting protection.

Then sleep dragged her back.

Giggling laughter. Sharp feet kicking. The wooden sides of the box are rough and splintery.

Pushing and shoving.

'Make room for me! Make room for me!'

'She's coming! She's coming! Be quick!'

A terrible confinement. Hardly room to breathe.

'Move your leg!'

'Be silent! She's coming!'

And Stephen reaches up and pulls the lid down.

Giggling, stifled laughter. No air. Tight space. Gasping.

'I can't breathe!'

'There's a little hole by the lock!'

'Let me near it. Please. Stephen. Please!'

'Are you dying, Samuel? Can't you breathe?'

More laughter, giggling laughter.

Distant sound from another world.

A voice calling, muffled and indistinct, as though far away.

'Samuel? Where are you? Samuel?'

A tiny cry.

'Help me! Help me!'

'Samuel? Where are you, dear?'

'Help me. . . .'

A hand covering the mouth. The sound of the voice choking into silence.

'Samuel? Where are you dear?' Then a long, diminishing call, echoing through the darkness, dying into silence:

'S . . a . . m . . u . . e . . l . . .'

The hand over the mouth tightening. The finger and thumb nipping the nose, the other fingers and the heel of the hand squeezing the mouth shut. The other arm wrapped round the body, hugging it towards him, holding it still.

A surge of power, of excitement. The best game ever.

'She's gone!' he whispers. 'We can get out now.'

A heavy weight, pushing him down. The body won't move.

'Samuel. Move! Samuel . . . I can't get out if you don't move.'

Terrible urgent actions. Forcing the lid upward. Air flooding in. Gasping for breath.

Squeezing past the body, pushing it sideways back into the chest. Staring down at the stricken face and the twisted form.

'Samuel? Get up, Samuel.'

Disbelief, fear, grief.

'Sam? Get up, Sam. Stop playing, Sam. Oh . . .' a whispered sob, 'S . . a . . m . . u . . e . . l . . .'

Turning away from the body in the box. Turning and running to the nursery stairs. Wanting to get away, to hide, to work out what to do next.

Running fast along the top landing. Seeing the door to the stairs slowly open and Miss Grey appearing, searching for Samuel, calling his name.

Dodging into the room and hiding from her. Squeezing behind the wardrobe, another favourite place, and holding the breath, terrified that she will find him.

And, later, the long scream from a distant room. The scream of discovery.

'Emma! Darling!'

Emma woke suddenly and found Harriet leaning over her, looking down at her.

'What?'

'You were having the most terrible dream.'

'Was I?'

'Unless you've been on the gin as well!'

'What happened?'

'You were screaming!'

'Sorry.'

'What was it?'

'A dream, I suppose.'

'It sounded awful. What was it about?'

Emma tried to remember, but she couldn't. Not then. Not at once.

2

Georgie Carver was sitting on an old wooden chair under an apple tree in the back garden.

The Carvers lived in one of the council houses on the estate at the end of the village. Built during the fifties, the houses were pebble-dashed, had metal frame windows and were all painted a dreary, uniform green. But they had long gardens and were surrounded by open countryside and Emma thought it would be quite a nice place to live, particularly if you were old and had nothing else to do all day but sit in a chair and let life slip by.

She had asked the way at the village post office-cum-shop and the woman behind the counter, who clearly knew exactly who she was, told her how to get into the back garden by going to the end of the block and along a narrow track that led to the fields behind.

'All the houses have back gates. You'll get in easy enough. It's Georgie you're after, is it? You'd please him if you took a quarter of toffees. He's got a sweet tooth, bless him.'

Emma thought it such an impressive sales pitch that she bought half a pound out of respect. The woman weighed them out on the post office scales and scooped them into a little white paper bag.

'He'll be glad of the company,' she said as she walked with her to the door. 'He's as right as rain, really. He just gets a bit muddled on account of his memory having gone.' Then she pointed her in the right direction and warned her to be careful at the bridge, 'because the traffic comes round that corner at a dreadful lick. We've complained to the council, but of course they do nothing about it. Nothing at all.'

Her route led past the doctor's house and she wondered whether Tim would be at home, but she didn't stop to enquire because she didn't want him to accompany her on her expedition to see Mr Carver.

The bridge was narrow and there was no pavement. But the only traffic she met was a woman with a pram and a boy on a bicycle. They both greeted her cheerfully and she felt sure that they also knew who she was.

It's like being visiting royalty, she thought.

The housing estate came into view at the top of a short hill and after she'd located the correct house number she went and looked for the side alley and made her way by it to the back gate.

Now she was standing in front of the old man and proffering the bag of toffees in her outstretched hand.

Georgie Carver ignored the offer and stared at her severely.

'And who are you?' he demanded.

'I'm a friend of your daughter,' Emma explained thinking that it wasn't so far from the truth.

'Florrie?'

'No, Lynda.'

The old man shook his head. 'I have so many memories,' he said. 'Florrie was best.'

'I'm staying at the Hall,' Emma said, feeling the conversation would be on shifting sand if she didn't quickly establish some common ground.

'I live here,' the old man told her, with a nod.

'It's very nice.'

He looked round. 'Aye. It's not bad. Did you see Florrie?'

'I'm not sure,' she answered, feeling she was losing ground again.

'You don't know Florrie?'

'Is she another daughter?'

'Daughter? She's the wife.'

'Oh, yes,' Emma said, frowning and looking uncomfortable. Lynda had never mentioned that her mother was also living there.

'Well? Did you see her?' the old man persisted.

'I think I did, yes,' Emma said, intuition telling her it might be better not to argue with him.

'I thought you would. She's just gone down to the pump.'

'Yes! That must be where I saw her.'

Mr Carver seemed pleased. He nodded and gave her a smile.

'That's right,' he said cheerfully. 'And you are . . . ?'

'Emma.'

'That's right, I remember now.' He clapped his hands and nodded in a satisfied way. 'I knew you at once. It's a while since you've been round. How's your mother? She and I used to walk out, you know. Before I met Florrie, of course.'

'Yes,' Emma said. She decided to sit on the grass in front of him. 'D'you want a toffee?' she asked, offering the bag once more.

'Go on then,' he said taking one. 'Florrie makes them. You'll never get a better toffee.'

'D'you remember Mr Westlake?' Emma ventured.

He frowned and looked away from her.

'Surely you do,' she said. 'Samuel Westlake. You used to work for him, didn't you, Mr Carver?'

'Aye. Happen,' he said quietly.

'Did you like working at the Hall?'

He just looked at her and blinked.

'Florrie should be back soon,' he said. 'We're going to pick brambles down at Lyke Lane and then she'll make a bramble pie. You can stop if you like. Florrie makes the best pastry in the entire country. People have always said so.'

They were silent for a while. Emma stared at the grass. The interview was proving more difficult than she'd expected. It seemed obvious to her that people were not right when they said that he had lost his memory, that he was forgetful. The opposite was nearer the truth. He had a head so packed with the past that his problem must be sifting through all the stored fragments and putting them into some kind of order. What Emma had to decide was whether a direct approach would work or if a subtle side attack would be better for releasing the information she was looking for.

'What was it you saw that day, up at the Hall?' she asked, choosing the direct approach first.

He looked at her and blinked. Then he frowned and rubbed his knees with his bony hands.

'They hurt,' he told her mournfully. 'I'm quite fit in myself, but the knees hurt. Mind, many of my contemporaries feel no pain at all. You know why?'

'No.'

'They're dead, that's why.'

'Is Mr Westlake dead?' Emma asked.

'Oh, he's been dead a long time. A long time.'

'They were twins, weren't they?'

'That's right. Twins. Our Jack and I – we're twins. But we don't look alike. D'you think we do?'

'Well,' she replied, trying to make a considered judgement, 'I've only seen your brother once but – I'd certainly say you were twins.'

'That's because we are. But people can tell us apart.'

'And the Westlake brothers . . . ?'

'Who?'

'Samuel and Stephen.'

'Ah now – I only ever knew one of them.'

'That was Samuel.'

He frowned and rubbed his knees.

'Was it?' he asked. His voice had stopped being animated and had taken on a sullen tone. 'Happen it was.'

'Tell me about the ghost,' Emma said.

He was silent again. Then he grinned.

'You've heard, have you? It was a bright autumn day. Or maybe it was spring. I was sweeping leaves up off the terrace. Or was it here that it happened? Maybe it was here?'

'I'm sure it was up at the Hall,' Emma prompted.

'That's right.' Now he started to recite a well-told tale, his voice singsong with familiarity. 'I ran and told Ettie Styles. There's a boy, I said, a young lad. He's trying to climb out of the window. You shut your noise, she said. But later she told the master. It was another day and I was digging. I did a lot of digging. George, he said. A word, he said. Now we never did see the master much. He never came out of the house and if he did, he kept to himself. So you could have knocked me down with a feather. What's this I hear, said he. Lies, is

194

it, George? And he had me dismissed. And I went to work for the Pease family.'

'But why? What had you done wrong?'

'Seen,' the old man replied, rubbing his knees again and staring at a distant scene perhaps not here but in the past.

'Seen what?' Emma asked.

'Too much,' he answered. Then he sighed and added in a quiet voice, 'And heard.'

Emma shivered involuntarily and turned and looked up at him.

'Heard? What did you hear?'

'That was my mistake, you see. It didn't do to tell.'

'What did you hear, Mr Carver?'

'Little high voice, screaming and screaming. "Let me out! Let me out! I can't breath! Let me out! Please Stephen. Let me out!' George Carver stopped speaking and brushed his cheek with his hand. Then he shook his head. 'I said: "It was you I was seeing, Mr Westlake. For you are Samuel and your poor dead brother, laid all these years in the grave-yard – he's Stephen. But how, Mr Westlake? How? How was I seeing your ghost when here you are as clear as day standing in front of me? For everyone knows you are Samuel Westlake and you cannot have a ghost if you are still alive, can you?'

'What does it mean, Mr Carver?' Emma whis-pered. George Carver shook his head. 'It didn't do to tell. He dismissed me. He found me another job. But he dismissed me. He said if I ever told there'd be trouble for me. Who would listen to the word of a simple labourer? So I didn't tell – not for years. Not till after he was dead.'

'What does it mean?'

'That Samuel had lain dead in the churchyard all these years and it was Stephen who was the master of Borthwick Hall.'

'What? I don't understand what you're saying.' Emma's heart was racing.

'You'd have to be a twin to understand,' the old man murmured, not looking at her. 'I knew at once. And he knew I knew, that's why he got shot of me.'

'Knew what?' Emma pleaded.

'Ah!' the old man said, 'it doesn't do to tell.' And although she tried to draw him further, Georgie Carver set his face and stared at the distant fields and never said another word to her.

3

It was teatime when she returned. As she turned into the back drive there was a plume of smoke hanging over the Hall. For a moment she had the absurd idea that maybe the house was on fire. That'd be one way to get rid of the ghosts! she thought and she was almost disappointed when, as the yard arch came into view, she saw a big bonfire blazing on the rough grass near to it.

Hank and Gary were piling pieces of timber and other refuse from the building work onto the fire from two wheelbarrows. They waved as she passed them.

Coming through the arch into the yard, she met Bill and Tom carrying a piece of the Victorian panelling towards one of the outhouses.

'What are you doing?' Emma called.

'Tidying up,' Tom answered. 'A safe ship is a tidy ship! Or whatever that stupid saying is.'

She walked beside them as they entered the out-house and went in with them.

'Have you finished then?' she asked.

'No! Have we hell!' Bill said as he and Tom added the panel to a stack of similar pieces, leaning against a wall.

The huge barn-like space was filled with furniture, most of it covered by dust sheets. There were lawn mowers and garden implements at the other end of the room. The air was filled with the scent of petrol and grass clippings and the old soily smells of a potting shed.

As they returned to the yard Emma asked them what they were going to do with the chest they'd found behind the panelling.

'We're leaving it in the nursery at the moment. Your mother says it looks nice. We've put it under one of the windows, like a sort of seat.'

'The Shawcrosses can decide where they want it, when they get back,' Tom added.

'Maybe they'll decide to get rid of it,' Emma said, speaking more to herself than to them.

'It's a good piece mind,' Bill said. 'I expect they'll want to keep it.'

'It should be worth a bit,' Tom said. 'Maybe they'll sell it.'

'Why would they?' Bill exclaimed. 'The one thing the Shawcrosses don't need is more money.'

'The rich can never resist having a bit more!' Tom observed, with a smile.

'You could take the chest,' Emma suggested. 'After all, they don't even know it exists.'

'Ah, but we're known as honest builders!' Bill said with a grin. 'That's how we get the work!'

'Besides,' Tom said, 'it's already been seen by all

of you lot – including Lynda Carver,' and he nodded across the yard to where Lynda Carver was climbing into her car. 'So, even if we wanted to, we'd never get away with it!'

'Hey, Lynda!' Bill shouted. 'You off?'

'I'm already late, so I can't stop,' Lynda called.

'What d'you want us to do with the key to this place?' Bill asked.

'Just leave it on the kitchen table. I'll deal with it in the morning. Oh, there you are, lady!' she said, seeing Emma. 'I've been looking high and low for you. Your boyfriend came to see you.'

'Boyfriend?' Bill said with a grin. He and Tom had picked up another piece of panelling from the diminishing pile in the yard and were carrying it towards the outhouse. 'Didn't take you long to get a boyfriend!' he called over his shoulder.

'He's not my boyfriend,' Emma said sullenly.

'Well, whatever he is, he said for you to ring him,' Lynda said. She started the engine and put the car into gear. 'Mind, don't go talking all hours on that telephone,' she continued, lowering the window, 'I'll be the one who'll get the blame if the Shawcrosses get back to a big bill.' Then she drove off with a wave.

Probably better if she doesn't know where I've been, Emma thought as she went into the house through the back door and, one thing's for sure, Georgie won't remember to tell her – though half the village will probably have done so before she reaches home.

She looked up the Ransom's number in the directory and then made the call on the telephone in the little sitting room, kneeling on the sofa and leaning on the back of it to reach the phone on the table.

It was Tim who answered but his voice sounded unfamiliar and Emma, not recognizing it, asked if she could speak to him.

'You are doing!' he said. 'Is that you, Emma?'

'How many other girls do you know?' she asked, trying to make a joke but sounding petulant instead.

'Not many.'

'I hear I missed you,' she said, trying again to be animated and cheerful.

'Yes.' His voice on the other hand seemed low and depressed.

'You all right?' she asked.

'Yeah, fine. Dad came home while I was out. On his own. Mum's staying down in hospital for longer than expected.'

'Oh, I'm sorry.'

Again she felt a ripple of guilt. As she didn't know Mrs Ransom she kept forgetting to enquire about her health.

'No, it's all right,' Tim was saying. 'Probably best really. They're doing more tests. Dad says it's a good sign. It's just that I know she hates being there. She should be out at the weekend. I'm going down to London with my aunt to bring her back.' He paused, then added, 'What are you doing tonight?'

'Nothing,' Emma said, then she remembered the big date with her prospective stepfather. 'Oh, I said I'd go out with Mother and . . . a friend.' When the voice at the other end of the phone didn't respond she added, 'Sorry!'

Tim cleared his throat. Then he said, 'Not to worry then.'

There was another long pause.

'Why did you ask?' Emma asked when she couldn't bear the silence any longer.

'I just wanted to see you.'

'Oh lord, Emmy!' a voice whispered in her head, 'I think he's after you!'

'How about tomorrow?' Emma said, too quickly, trying to concentrate on Tim and to blot out the other voice.

'Yes, maybe,' he said, stumbling over the words in his anxiety. 'I'm not sure. If I can. Maybe . . .'

'Well, it was only a suggestion,' Emma snapped, irritated by his indecisiveness. Then at once she wished she hadn't. Another pause followed. 'You are all right, Tim, are you?' she asked.

'Yeah. I'm fine. I just hate it when Mum's in hospital and we're all miles away from her.'

'Maybe you should go down to London sooner.'

'I'll see what Jane says.'

'Who's Jane?' She felt a sudden twinge of jealousy.

'My aunt,' he replied. 'Oh, by the way, about the Borthwick murder . . .'

'What about it?'

'I found Mother's notes in her desk. Apparently the Westlakes went away to Scotland soon after the death of Stephen and they stayed away for almost a year.' He sounded more cheerful now he was thinking about other things. His voice became brighter and lighter as he rattled off the facts he had discovered. 'There were relatives of Mrs Westlake who had a house near Dundee and they went and lived with them. The father came back to York on his own for the trial and stayed at the County Hotel. It was said at the trial that Samuel Westlake, the remaining son, had given evidence under oath to the magistrates, but that he was considered too young to appear in the witness box himself. He was only eight, you see. His evidence – delivered by the magistrate – is included in the report of the trial.'

'He wouldn't want to say much,' Emma said, half-remembering without realizing her dream of the night before.

'Oh, he did!' Tim said, sounding surprised at her remark. 'It was Samuel Westlake's evidence that was the centre of the trial.'

'Really?' Emma said, puzzled.

'He witnessed the whole thing.'

'Yes!' Emma exclaimed, the memory of the dream surging into her consciousness. 'Yes, of course! He saw everything. Of course. . . . But I'm surprised he'd want to tell – and anyway, how would what he knew condemn Miss Grey? I'd have thought it'd have done just the opposite.'

'Have you seen a report of the trial?' Tim asked, sounding confused.

'No, no!' Emma said hurriedly. 'But I've been trying to work things out. Go on, please.'

'Samuel told the magistrate he had been hiding behind one of the curtains in the nursery when it happened. He saw the governess push his brother, Stephen, into the chest and slam the lid. He said she stuffed cloth over the keyhole of the latch and that she sat on the chest while the kid was screaming inside. . . .'

'No!' Emma exclaimed. 'That isn't true.'

'That's what he said.'

Emma's mind was racing. She felt as though she were in the witness stand herself. All that was being said was a lie. She knew the truth. But how could she prove it? Who would believe her?

A flaw in the story suddenly occurred to her and she leapt at it triumphantly.

'If Samuel was there at the time – and in the very same room where the murder took place – then why didn't he go and stop Miss Grey?'

'What could he have done? He was only an eight year old. She was a grown woman.'

'They were strong little boys. He could have dragged her off the chest easily. Then he had only to get the lid open and Stephen would have been free to help him. Between them they'd have been more than a match for her.'

'He said he was too scared. He said he knew she would put him in the chest as well.'

'All right then – why didn't he run for help? There must have been other servants in the house. He could have got along the landing and down the stairs to the hall in seconds. There'd be bound to have been a cook in the kitchen. . . . Men working in the gardens. . . . There'd have been lots of people about. They wouldn't all have been out hunting.'

'The defence made a lot of that point.'

'So?'

'They were told that if Samuel had left his hiding place behind the curtain Miss Grey could have easily caught him before he reached the door. He believed that she would then have dragged him to the chest and pushed him in as well.'

'But while she was catching Samuel, Stephen could have pushed open the lid and escaped,' Emma protested.

'There's a metal hasp on the chest. The lid would have been held closed by it.'

'This is all a load of nonsense, Tim!' Emma exclaimed. 'You mean they convicted her on that

202

evidence? The word of a child who wasn't even in the court? Who wasn't there to be cross examined? If he had been he could have been . . . made to tell the truth.'

'Don't get so worked up, Emma.'

'He was lying. I don't know why, but he was lying.' She was so indignant now that her voice had risen and she was shouting into the telephone.

'Hey! Calm down,' she heard Tim say in an infuriatingly calm and almost mocking voice. 'It's just history. Something that happened ages ago. Don't get so worked up about it.'

Emma was shaking and sweating. The hand not holding the phone was clenched so tightly that her nails were cutting into the palm.

'But it isn't fair . . .' she yelled.

'It's interesting though, don't you think? And anyway, there's nothing we can do about it now. We can't put the clocks back. We can't un-hang the governess!'

'She was condemned to death on a lie,' Emma exclaimed. Tim's complacency was beginning to madden her.

'It wasn't just the boy's evidence that did it. I told you. The governess really condemned herself. When she was called to the witness box, she refused to say anything in her own defence. Not a single word did she utter. She answered basic questions about her name, her age and her status and nothing else.'

'Why?'

'I don't know, Emma!' Tim shouted, losing his temper with her. 'I wasn't there, was I?'

No, she thought. You may not have been, but I was. And soon after she brought the conversation

203

to a close, saying that she had to go and get ready
for the evening.

DIARY

Supposing . . .

*There are twin sons. One called Stephen, the other
Samuel. Stephen is a bully; he's always playing tricks
and being nasty. Samuel is quieter. They have a governess
(Miss Grey). She can only just cope with them both –
but she much prefers Samuel (the quiet one) and actually
dislikes Stephen. (She has beaten him and pulled his hair
in her anger). One day when they are playing (and by
playing I think I mean their usual game – goading and
frightening Miss Grey. Hiding from her; jumping out at
her; running through the house, dazzling her with reflected
light, giggling and whispering horrible things. . . . Always
with Stephen as the ringleader – in fact he probably
frightens Samuel as much as he frightens Miss G. and
Samuel has to go along with him mainly for his own
safety, because if Miss G. wasn't there for Stephen to
intimidate he'd probably set his sights on Samuel instead).
Anyway, one day when they're playing they both hide in
the chest in the nursery. Samuel gets scared and starts
shouting out for Miss Grey. Stephen – just playing and
not wanting them to be discovered – puts his hand over
his brother's mouth and nose to stop the noise. . . . He
holds on . . . and on . . . until Samuel has suffocated.
(How long would that take? Maybe he did it for a long
time? But he was excited – and it was only a game they
were playing. I'm sure of that. I mean I really know that's
how it was). Anyway – Stephen kills Samuel. But they
are such identical-looking twins that when Miss G. finds
the body she doesn't know which one of them is dead –
and neither do his parents and Stephen decides to be Samuel,*

204

because no one would ever believe Samuel would have killed his brother but Stephen could quite easily have done so. (In fact he did – but by accident and not on purpose). Also Samuel gets all the love – and Stephen is always blamed for everything. And Samuel is popular with his parents – while Stephen is considered the black sheep. . . . And Samuel is always believed by his parents – and Stephen never is. So when Stephen claims he's Samuel, they are prepared to believe whatever he says – even that it was Miss Grey who killed his brother.

Stephen – now accepted by everyone as Samuel – never really meant to kill his brother. But he has to live with the fact for the rest of his life. And maybe, later, he'll even feel some guilt for what he did to the governess. Maybe it is a long time before he finds out that she was hanged for the murder. (They wouldn't tell a little eight year old something like that. Not when he's obviously already in a state of shock).

That's it! Maybe he really was in a state of shock. He hid in the top bedroom for nearly two days. Of course! He was probably terrified about what had happened – about what he'd done. He put the blame on Miss Grey, because he believed that otherwise he'd be the one who'd be punished.

(Just read this through and it occurs to me that even if the parents knew that Samuel was really Stephen – they wouldn't say. They wouldn't want to lose both their sons. To avoid that they'd gladly go along with his story and would accuse Miss Grey themselves – because they'd need someone to take the rap. A scapegoat. Maybe that's why they stayed away in Scotland for a year . . . to let the dust settle so that when Samuel returned with them (really Stephen) no one would start asking awkward questions).

But Miss Grey. Miss Grey! Why didn't you defend yourself??

Finally, when Georgie Carver came on the scene years and years later, he somehow KNEW what had happened. He knew that Mr Westlake was really Stephen and not Samuel. Stephen got scared and got rid of him and warned him not to say anything. . . . And poor, simple Mr Carver kept it bottled up all his life until old Mr Westlake died and by then everyone thought George was potty and they didn't bother to listen to him.

Next question: How did Mr Carver stumble on so much? Why was he haunted? And – why am I haunted? Why us two?

Emma put down her biro and rubbed the scratch on her cheek gently. It was itching, which probably meant it was getting better.

Then picking up her biro again she leant over the exercize book lying on the bed beside her and added to the bottom of the page:

Maybe he was haunted because he, like the ghost – like Mr Westlake also – was a twin. Maybe it takes a twin to know how a twin will behave.

But that doesn't explain my haun

Emma stopped writing again in the middle of the word.

With a terrible convulsive shudder she remembered her other dream of the previous evening. It hit her like a physical blow on the forehead. The memory actually stunned her. It made her gasp and little bright lights flashed at the back of her eyes.

Then the room started to sway and move and no matter how hard she clung to the bedspread she felt herself falling sideways into a great spinning vortex.

As she hit the floor and sank into unconsciousness she heard again the high echoing laughter that had haunted her all her life.

'Poor Emmy!' her voice said. 'Now you're beginning to understand, aren't you?'

Eleven

1

When Harriet came up to change for the evening she found Emma lying on the floor, apparently dozing.

'Darling, what on earth are you doing?' she exclaimed coming into the room from the nursery stairs.

'I fell off the bed,' Emma said, waking with a start and sitting up, rubbing her temple. She could feel a slight lump where she must have hit her head on the floor. She looked around, puzzled, trying to recall what had happened. She remembered writing in her diary and later the room beginning to spin.

I must have fainted, she thought. I've never done that before.

Her breathing was tight and wheezy again and she couldn't stop her body trembling.

'You're going to have an awful bruise,' Harriet said, peering at her. Then she felt her forehead. 'I'm sure you're running a temperature now. I'd better call the doctor.'

'No. It's nothing serious!' Emma stopped her going, speaking urgently. 'Honestly, you don't need to. It's just the heat I expect and this stupid asthma. I'll be OK if I lie down for a few minutes.'

She struggled up from the floor with Harriet's help and flopped down on the side of the bed.

'Well, one thing's certain. You can't go out this evening,' Harriet told her.

'Yes, I can,' Emma protested. 'I must. It's important.'

'Of course it isn't. We can go another day.'

'But I don't want to spoil it for you,' Emma said, then she surprised them both by beginning to cry.

'Darling?' Harriet said gently, sitting down beside her and putting an arm round her shoulder. 'It's all right. We can go out with Simon any evening.'

'But I have to meet him. He wants to ask me if he can marry you. . . .'

Harriet laughed lightly and hugged her.

'Put like that it's no wonder your asthma came back!' she said.

'I'll be all right, honestly I will.'

'You're not going out like this,' Harriet insisted. 'No arguments, OK?'

'I'm ruining everything.'

'Emma! Darling! It's no big deal. There'll be lots of other chances for us all to have dinner together.'

'You must go though. You will, won't you?'

'No! I'm not leaving you alone here.'

'I'll be all right.'

'I don't think this place is good for you. You're spending too much time moping about on your own. It was a bad idea your coming up here. You'd have been far better staying in Strand-on-the-Green, with Muti.'

'I like it here.'

209

'Well, something's brought your asthma back. Probably anxiety!'

'Why would I be anxious?' Emma asked.

'I expect it's because of Simon,' Harriet replied with a grim look.

'Is that what you think?'

'You've never liked any of my boyfriends,' Harriet said.

'I haven't usually, I admit. But I'm going to try really hard with this one.'

Harriet looked at her and laughed.

'Darling!' she exclaimed.

'What?'

'You make it sound such an ordeal!' She smiled. 'I do love you, you know.'

'Mother, please!' Emma groaned with embarrassment, sounding more like her old self.

'I do wish you'd stop calling me that,' Harriet sighed.

'What?'

'Mother – it sounds so unfriendly.'

'But you are my mother,' Emma protested.

'I know. It's just – somehow it sounds so distant.'

'So what d'you want me to call you?'

'I don't know,' Harriet shrugged. 'You used to call me Mum or Mummy.'

'That was ages ago – when I was a child.'

Harriet stared at her thoughtfully.

'I suppose that's it, is it? You're not a child any longer. Maybe you should call me Harriet.'

'Mother!' Emma exclaimed, embarrassed again. Then she smiled, shyly. 'Just go and get ready, please, and GO OUT. All I want to do is sleep. So there's no point you being here.'

Suddenly she wanted to be on her own. There

was so much that she needed to think about, so much that she wanted to digest.

But Harriet had other ideas.

'I tell you what,' she said pulling down the covers on the bed. 'You get into bed and I'll phone Simon. He can come here for supper and maybe we'll go to the pub if you seem OK later.'

Emma realized that her mother was changing her plans specially for her. It seemed churlish therefore to argue any more. At least once she was in bed she'd have some time to herself.

She started to take off her clothes and, as she did so, caught sight of her reflection in the mirror on the dressing table.

'I'm sorry about the tattoo,' she said, remembering the row they'd had in the car on the way back from the doctor's and wanting now to make amends – to repay Harriet's kindness towards her with a gesture of her own.

'I'm very angry about it,' Harriet exclaimed, reacting at once. 'It was such a stupid thing to do, Em!' Then she shrugged. 'Oh, well! You're the one who's going to have to live with it. Why should I care?'

'I don't really know why I did it now.'

'Oh, I do!' Harriet assured her. 'If I'd told you that I wanted you tattooed from head to toe, you wouldn't have dreamed of having one!'

'No! It wasn't like that,' Emma said crawling into bed and settling back against the pile of pillows that Harriet had placed for her. 'I needed something . . . personal. A distinguishing feature. . . .' Then, without hesitating, she added, 'What happened to my twin?'

As she asked the question she saw Harriet, who

211

was picking up her discarded clothes from the floor and folding them, flinch. There was a moment's pause while Harriet composed her features into an amused, quizzical look. Then she said;

'Twin?' trying to make the word sound inconsequential.

'Yes,' Emma replied, staring at her thoughtfully. 'I did have a twin, didn't I?'

'Oh, I see!' Harriet said. And, still holding Emma's jeans, she sat down on the dressing table stool. 'Muti's been telling you things, has she?'

Emma frowned, then nodded.

'Yes, Muti. Muti told me,' she lied. 'What happened to my twin?'

'She didn't tell you everything then?' her mother said, a bitter note creeping into her voice. 'She left out the juicy bits? How unlike her.'

'No. Don't blame Muti,' Emma said, feeling guilty for having involved her grandmother so shamefully in the lie.

'She knew I didn't want you told,' Harriet said, quietly.

'But – why?'

'It's the past, Emma.'

'And yet sometimes the past won't go away. It hasn't for us.'

'Talking about it won't help.'

'It might,' Emma whispered. 'It's worth a try. Please tell me what happened. Please, Mum.'

'She was stillborn. . . .'

'She?'

'Your twin. It was another girl.'

'A girl,' Emma sighed. Then she nodded. 'Did you know you were carrying twins?'

'Yes.'

'Did my father?'

'Of course.'

Emma quietly digested this information.

'Might it have been easier for him, d'you think, if you'd only been expecting one baby?'

'Easier?'

'I mean – would he have stayed with us?'

'Oh! No,' Harriet said, realizing the direction of her thoughts. 'It wasn't the number of babies that he objected to. He didn't want any.'

Emma frowned. 'How did she die?'

Harriet shrugged and continued to fold the clothes and put them neatly on the chair.

'They say being born is a very risky business,' she said, with her back turned towards Emma. She paused for a moment, straightening up and staring into the distance, lost in memory. 'I knew something was wrong. I couldn't do anything about it. But I knew. I knew.'

'Was I born first?' Emma asked.

'Oh, yes,' her mother told her, sounding surprised by her question. 'You were an easy birth. But then Kate . . . wouldn't come. It was as if she didn't want to be born. She was in the wrong position. We always knew it might be tricky.'

'Kate?' Emma gasped.

'That's what I was going to call her,' Harriet said and when she turned and looked at Emma there were tears in her eyes.

2

Emma dressed in the dark. She had heard Harriet come to bed at least half an hour before. She didn't want to put on the light for fear of waking her. She wished she had a torch. Not for now, not for her room, but for later when she was downstairs.

She went to the chest of drawers and selected a thick sweater. She was glad Harriet had insisted she should bring it. Harriet had said they were going to the north and it was bound to be freezing up there. It wasn't freezing of course, it was the middle of a heatwave and even outside it would probably still be warm, but she was glad of the sweater. It comforted her. It was soft and familiar and smelt of home.

Emma had spent the evening lying in bed, dozing and waking fitfully. Harriet had come several times to see that she was all right. She had refused to go out and had even stopped Simon from visiting the house.

'We'll see him another night,' she'd said. She seemed quite worried about Emma and said that if she wasn't better in the morning then she was definitely calling the doctor.

Gradually, as the evening had ticked away and she'd waited for Harriet to be safely in bed, Emma had formed her plan. She knew what she was going to do. She just hoped she had the courage and strength to see it through.

Now, fully clothed and wearing her soft-soled trainers, she tiptoed to the door and opened it quietly.

Harriet's bedroom door, immediately opposite, was wide open. She must have left it like that so that she would hear if Emma needed her in the night. Even the sound of the latch moving woke her. As Emma watched, she saw the bedside light flick on in the room across the passage and she heard her mother call:

214

'Em? Is that you?'

Emma inched the door closed again and hurried back to bed. She got in, fully clothed, and pulled the covers over her. A moment later the door opened and Harriet, lit from behind, appeared in the opening, listening and looking towards the bed.

'Emma?' she whispered. 'Are you all right?'

Emma didn't answer and feigned sleep with slow, heavy breathing.

After a few moments Harriet went quietly out again, leaving the door slightly open.

So Emma waited for another seemingly endless time. Then she started again.

First she crossed and pushed her door closed. She had hoped to go down the stairs at the end of the corridor, but she didn't dare risk disturbing Harriet again. She could hear her snoring quietly across the passage, but knew that the slightest noise would wake her.

The alternative was one that she dreaded. She had hoped to avoid spending longer than necessary in the nursery. Now she would have to start off by passing through it. Opening the door to the nursery stairs she took out the key and placed it carefully in the pocket of her jeans. She didn't trust any of them and she didn't want to be locked out of her room on her return. Her plan depended on her getting in and out of her room without Harriet ever knowing that she had left it. Then, without allowing herself to think about it – like jumping into cold water – she ran quickly and quietly down the steep steps to the room below.

The nursery was bathed in pale moonlight from the long windows. She saw the chest at once. The builders had placed it under one of the windows in exactly the position it had occupied in her dream. The sight of it made her hesitate. She stopped running for a moment – wondering how they could have known so precisely where it belonged. The silver light from the moon reflected on its polished surface, making it glow in the dark. She walked slowly towards it, listening for the laughter or the banging, or the terrible scream.

Only silence accompanied her as she dared to move the iron hasp and lift the lid. She was surprised how heavy the wood was. It was going to take all her strength to accomplish what she was setting out to do.

The inside of the box was empty. It smelt of wood and dust and old dampness.

She closed the lid again. At the last moment it slipped from her fingers and slammed with a sharp *bang*. She gasped and started back, listening intently. But the only sound that followed the disturbance was her own heavy, wheezy breath and her beating heart.

She turned and ran quickly out of the room. The door to the Games Room was wide open. The smell of new paint filled her nostrils. She ran to the opening and looked in, framed in the doorway like a shadow.

Perhaps I'm a ghost to the ghosts, she thought, and she shivered with apprehension.

'Move, Emma,' she whispered to herself. 'Don't push your luck!'

She ran lightly to the head of the stairs and then down them to the half landing. Her she paused again, waiting and listening.

'Where are they?' she asked herself. 'What are they doing?'

216

The silence was almost worse than the expected haunting. She felt as if she were being watched from all the dark shadows; she was certain that somewhere they were waiting for her. The atmosphere was tense with anticipation; she imagined the boys hugging themselves gleefully, loving her agitation, revelling in her fear.

She ran fast down the centre flight of stairs and when she was nearly at the bottom she missed a step and tripped, falling heavily and sprawling across the black and white tiled floor.

Breathing laboriously, she crouched on her hands and knees, listening again. The temptation to shout out was growing in her. She needed to know where they were.

'No! No,' she whispered, willing herself to be silent.

Taking a deep breath, she scrambled to her feet and ran for the servants' door.

Once in the back hall she felt a degree of relief. She went into the kitchen and picked up the outhouse key from the centre of the table, where Bill must have placed it, as instructed by Lynda. She had worried that her mother might have moved it during the evening. The fact that she hadn't struck Emma as a good omen.

'So far, so good!' she murmured. Then, crossing to the cooker, she collected a box of kitchen matches.

She unlocked the back door and let herself out into the yard. The air was cool here and heavy with summer scents. As she ran across the yard an owl swooped overhead, screeching at the night.

She let herself into the outhouse and fumbled on the wall beside the door. She thought, as her mother's room was facing away from the yard, that she could allow herself the comfort of some light. But she couldn't find a switch. She struck a match and by its light, located one. But when a row of bulbs went on along the full length of the outhouse, the light was so bright that she took fright and immediately extinguished them again.

'I'll work by match light,' she told herself.

She made for the end of the room where, earlier in the day, she had seen that all the lawnmowers and wheelbarrows were stored. She chose the largest of the wheelbarrows and then, searching amongst the lawnmowers, she found a can of petrol. She put the can into the wheelbarrow and pushed it out into the yard.

She went through the arch and left the can of petrol on the side of the drive near to where the builders' bonfire was still smouldering and glowing with dull red embers.

She pulled the wheelbarrow backwards up the steps to the back door, then turned and pushed it swiftly along the corridor and out into the main hall.

Again she stopped, listening. The house was so quiet that the silence seemed to hum around her.

She turned her back on the stairs and dragged the wheelbarrow up after her as far as the half-landing. The exertion was affecting her breathing. Her chest felt tight and her shoulders were hunched as she dragged at the air, trying to fill her lungs. She rested for a moment, half sitting on the side of the barrow.

Out of the corner of her eye she thought she saw a shadow move, up on the landing above her. She looked quickly round.

Someone – someone tall and slim – was leaning over the banister rail, looking down at her.

'Miss Grey?' she whispered. 'Is it you?'

The figure pulled back slightly, as if surprised to hear her voice.

'I've come to help you,' Emma whispered.

The figure remained leaning against the banister, so shadowy and indistinct that Emma was only half sure that there was anyone there at all.

She waited for a long time then, when the figure didn't move, she started to pull the wheelbarrow on up the second flight of stairs towards the landing. Once there, she looked along the length of the banister, searching for the person. But whoever it had been, if indeed there'd been anyone, had now disappeared.

'A shadow,' Emma said aloud, hoping to comfort herself with the sound of her own voice.

The silence that followed crackled with potential. Then out of it, sighing like a breath of breeze she heard a voice calling:

'Samuel,' it said, with a sad cadence. 'Samuel, where are you dear?'

Emma turned and ran along the landing to the open nursery door, pushing the barrow in front of her.

As soon as she entered the room she saw that the chest lid was open. She had closed it of course. She knew she had. She remembered the sound as the lid had slipped out of her fingers and slammed. The sight of it now – open – filled her less with fear than with anticipation. It was a relief that they were here.

Leaving the wheelbarrow by the door, she tiptoed across the room.

219

Moonlight was flooding in from the long windows.

Lying in a crumpled heap in the chest, his white face hideously distorted, was a young boy with a mass of black curly hair. As Emma saw the body she heard again the long, terrified scream that she had heard here in this room when she had first seen the chest.

Hands with lace-edged wrists leaned on the side of the chest in front of her.

'Samuel! What have we done to you? Oh, Samuel! My poor! My little one!' The terrible lamentation of despair. The broken sigh of grief.

Miss Grey knew it was Samuel, Emma thought. She knew that Stephen was alive. She was never taken in by the deception.

'So why didn't you defend yourself?' Emma asked, speaking loudly, indignantly. She drew back, watching, waiting, determined to know. The hands on the side of the chest were her own, the arms covered by the thick sweater.

Looking once more into the chest she saw, as she knew she would, that it was empty. She shut the lid and went back across the room to collect the wheelbarrow.

As soon as her back was turned she heard the knocking. It was coming from the chest. But she knew it was an illusion. She had just seen, with her own eyes, that it was empty.

She pushed the barrow back across the room.

In front of her the lid of the chest burst open and a boy jumped out, waving his hands in the air and pulling a hideous face. As she made a grab for him, he dodged out of the way and she fell heavily against the side of the chest.

Looking in once more she saw a figure crouched inside. Slowly the head was raised and Emma was staring into her own eyes. The figure in the chest was herself. She was looking at herself. But something was different. There was no scratch on her cheek. And, as she watched, the figure pulled open the neck of her shirt collar. There was no small black star on her shoulder; there was no tattoo.

'Kate?' Emma whispered.

'Emmy!' the figure sang the name.

'What do you want?' Emma asked.

'Emmy,' her twin sang the name again. The voice was the one Emma had heard on occasions all through her life. The same mocking tone, the same intimate familiarity.

'What do you want?' Emma shouted.

'Losing your temper, Emmy dear? Clever little Emmy. You'll never be free of me now.'

'It wasn't my fault, Kate. What happened wasn't my fault.'

The figure in the chest beckoned to her.

Slowly, mesmerized by the beckoning finger, Emma climbed into the chest and crouched down. There was just room for her inside. But if the lid were closed, the claustrophobia would be terrible.

'Got you! Got you! Got you!' a boy's voice screamed.

And, as the lid slammed down on top of Emma, she heard another voice wailing;

'Help me! Help me! . . .'

'Samuel? Where are you, dear?'

'I can't breathe. Please, Stephen. Please.'

'Samuel. . . . Where are you dear? S . . a . . m . . u . . e . . l.'

'NO!' Emma shouted, turning within the tight

space, so that she was facing upwards. She placed her hands against the underside of the wooden lid and pushed. It wouldn't move. She was trapped. The iron hasp must have fallen over the catch. She was locked in.

There was no air. No light.

'Help me,' she gasped. 'Someone, h .. e .. l .. p m .. e!'

'Samuel, dear?' Miss Grey called from the open world, beyond the box.

'MISS GREY,' Emma shouted. 'Help me! Please, please. . . . HELP ME!'

'It isn't very nice, is it, Emmy dear?' a voice murmured, very close to her.

'Kate,' Emma gasped. 'Why are you doing this?'

'It's . . . a game.'

'No. It isn't Kate. You must stop this now. You must. Why? Why, Kate? What is it you blame me for?'

'You lived,' the voice said.

Terrible panic seized her. If she didn't get out soon, she never would. Turning in the confined space she discovered a tiny hole in the wall of the chest. It was beside the metal lock. She remembered now that Stephen had found it on that dreadful night. That's how he had managed to breathe. Through the hole she could see a minute portion of the room. The door leading to the landing was partially in view. There was a figure standing in the doorway, staring at the box. She recognized the tall, slim figure she had seen at the top of the stairs. The person didn't move. The person was allowing her to die.

'Miss Grey!' Emma shouted. 'Help me. You must help me. You must this time. You must.' Then she pleaded with the figure. 'If you help me, I'll stop all this. Help me?'

There was a desperate moment of silence. Then she heard quick, light steps as the figure came towards the chest. The view through the tiny hole in the wood was obscured. Someone was standing immediately in front of it. For a long moment nothing happened then, above her head, Emma heard the metal hasp being lifted from the catch.

She saw the light at the end of the tunnel. She swam towards it. Cool, clean air was coming towards her. With one final, mighty push, the lid opened and, gasping and panting, Emma leaned against the side of the oak chest, looking out into the room.

'Thank you,' she called and somewhere she thought she could hear a woman, crying.

'You were innocent, Miss Grey. I know what happened. Stephen was playing and he suffocated Samuel. Then he was too frightened to own up and he put the blame on you. You knew, didn't you? But you took the blame. I don't know why.' Emma cried. 'I don't know why.'

As she climbed out of the chest she looked back and saw her twin staring at her from inside the chest. Emma offered her her hand, to help her out. But the twin didn't move. She knew she was dead, the staring eyes told her so.

'I'm sorry,' Emma said and she closed the lid.

Later she dragged the chest across the floor to where she had left the wheelbarrow. Lifting one end of it she balanced it on the side of the barrow and shuffled and pushed until it was lodged in place, jutting out precariously in front.

She started to push the barrow towards the door

and out along the landing to the staircase. But the chest was too big and too heavy and after only a few steps it started to slide sideways off the barrow. Crying with frustration, Emma pulled it back on top.

When she arrived at the stairs she had to go backwards down them, allowing the wheel of the barrow to drop from step to step. It took her an age to reach the hall floor, but somehow she managed it. She forced herself to succeed. She knew it was the most important thing she was ever likely to do in her life.

The journey to the bonfire took half the night. Three times the chest fell off the barrow, and three times she tugged and pulled it back into place.

When she reached the fire she doused the chest with petrol from the can she had taken there earlier. She stood the chest on its narrow end. It was as tall as her. Then, to be sure, she poured more petrol over it. The fumes were acrid and caught in the back of her throat. Finally she slowly toppled the chest away from her so that it fell onto the glowing embers.

Nothing happened. She was afraid that the weight of the chest had flattened out the embers and smothered the fire. . . . She thought she had failed. Now, after all the effort, after all the hours of toil and anguish, she thought the chest wasn't going to ignite.

She was searching in the dark for the box of kitchen matches when, with a deafening sound, the chest exploded into shattering light. The force of the eruption and the searing heat of the flames knocked her off her feet. She fell back onto the damp

224

grass, jolting her back and twisting her neck as her head struck the ground.

The last thing she remembered were the flames leaping up into the dark sky and the crackling, chattering, consuming sound of the fire.

PART THREE

LONDON
(Strand-On-The-Green)

Dear Tim,

Sorry I left without saying goodbye. It was all a bit rushed. I'm not sure what you'll have been told and my version of the story will be about as unlikely as everyone else's. But I will try to explain.

Apparently on my last night at Borthwick Mum woke in the early hours and found my bed empty. The door to the nursery steps was open so she assumed that I must have gone down there. There was no sign of me anywhere in the main house and so, because she was already worried (I'd been quite ill earlier) she went down to the kitchen to see if I was there. The back door was open which led her to the yard and from the yard to the bonfire that the builders had started the day before.

According to her there were sheets of flame reaching as high as the roof of the house and I was lying on the grass unconscious some way from it. There was also a terrible stink of petrol.

I don't really remember any of this. Which may be a handy way of avoiding the truth or simply – as everyone seems to think – that I was having a breakdown!

229

The chest that the builders had found (do you remember? You saw it. It was you who told me it was probably the one the little Westlake boy had been found dead in.) Anyway, it was burning away like anything. I'd somehow managed to get it down from the nursery – using a wheelbarrow.

Mum wasn't angry about the chest – not at the time. Though since, she's gone ape about it. 'It was probably worth a fortune . . .' 'It belonged to the Shawcross family . . .' 'What will they do when they find out . . .?' etc. etc. You can no doubt imagine the scene! It was Lynda Carver who suggested that they shouldn't be told. She pointed out that what they didn't know about they'd never miss. It was really nice of her. But you know I suspect that she believed more of her father's story than she admitted. I think she knew why I had to burn it. I think she was glad that I did. And I did have to burn it, Tim. It was the only way to stop the haunting. I still believe that.

Anyway, I've been rushed down to London and am staying with my grandmother in her house at Strand-on-the-Green while Mum finishes off the work up there – and no doubt sees a lot of Simon Wentworth. But that's another story and will only complicate matters if I go into it now.

Everything is still a bit of a muddle for me but in a way I feel more peaceful now than I have done for ages. Actually being up at Borthwick was like one of those weird therapies for me. (You know the scene – primal screaming and all that stuff! There are constant documentaries about those groups on TV – usually when you want to watch a good film! – and I've always thought they were a load of nonsense.) But this did help – mainly because Mum and I were able to talk in a way that we've always avoided in the past. But also because I faced up to things that I

230

haven't wanted to – not ever. Well, I may have wanted to – but I've never had the courage.

What really happened to me up there I'll never know. But I will always remember this summer; the summer of the haunting. It was the year I gave myself a tattoo and the year I discovered about Kate and the year that I met you.

I hope the news is better about your mother and that the enclosed notes taken from the diary I was keeping while I was up there (just some thoughts I had about the murder at the Hall) will be of interest to her.

By the way, I think I know why Miss Grey didn't speak up at her trial. I think she did feel responsible – guilty, even. I think that when Stephen ran from the chest, leaving Samuel dead, he closed the lid. I think Miss Grey glimpsed him, and believed him when he said he was Samuel. She thought that Samuel had left Stephen in the oak chest . . . and she didn't do anything. She just stood at the door and stared at the chest, and didn't go to the child's aid. Because she WANTED Stephen dead as much as she believed Samuel wanted it. Then, when she opened the lid – she realized that the wrong child had died. Miss Grey really loved Samuel. Maybe if you really love someone you do recognize them. Maybe. . . .

But, like I say, it's all a great muddle. Let's hope your mother can work it out. It'll make a great book one day. Tell her to hurry up and get on with it – or the dreaded, soon to be stepfather, Simon Wentworth will write it first.

If you're ever in London, get in touch—

231

'Emmy!' a voice whispered, somewhere close to her.

Emma stopped writing and looked around, holding her breath.

'Little Emmy!' the voice cooed in her head.

'Ah!' Emma sighed. 'I suppose I always knew . . .'

'What?'

'That sooner or later I'd hear from you again.'

'Did you hope you'd got rid of me?'

'I wasn't sure. Yes – and then again – no.'

'But you did want to?'

'Oh, yes,' Emma replied, emphatically.

'Wouldn't you miss me at all?'

'Probably,' Emma sighed. She suddenly felt very weary. 'Yes, Kate, I'd probably miss you, in a way. After all, I've never known a time when you weren't with me.'

'And yet you wanted to get rid of me, didn't you. Like you did the others. You did, didn't you? You did!'

Emma got up without answering and walked away.

'Well, I'm still here, Emmy dear,' the voice crowed with gleeful satisfaction. 'Are you scared?

You are, aren't you, now I'm back. You're scared all over again.'

'No,' Emma replied firmly. 'We're going to have to learn to live together, you and I. It's our only hope. When I was born, you came with me – only you left your body behind. Your body died, you see, during the birth . . . Stillborn, they call it. Poor Kate!'

'Clever aren't you?' the voice mocked. 'You think yourself so clever. When did you work that out?'

'When I realized what had happened to Samuel and Stephen.'

'What did happen?'

'The same that happened to us. Samuel joined Stephen when they were in the chest – it was as if they were being reborn. When Samuel died, he took Stephen's body to share – just as you took mine.'

'So,' Kate crooned in her most singsong, mocking voice, 'you're probably much more me than you are yourself! Poor Emmy!' and she laughed lightly.

But Emma shook her head and turned and stared at her reflection in the bedroom mirror. 'I don't think so, Kate,' she said quietly.

'Oh, you may be able to see your body,' her dead twin snapped, sounding angry now. The anger made her voice vicious. 'But who are you really, Emmy? That's what you'll never know. All the time it could be me – and you'll never be certain. Not ever . . .'

But Emma only smiled. I'm the one with the tattoo, she thought. She pulled back her shirt and revealed the small black star on her shoulder.

'That's me!' she whispered.